Disappearing

Wetlands

DISAPPEARING WETLANDS

Helen J. Challand, Ph.D.

Technical Consultant
Milton W. Weller, Ph.D.
Professor of Wildlife Ecology
Department of Wildlife and Fisheries
Texas A&M University

ϞP CHILDRENS PRESS®
CHICAGO

A production of B&B Publishing, Inc.

Project Editor: Jean Blashfield Black
Designer: Elizabeth B. Graf
Cover Design: Margrit Fiddle
Artist: Valerie A. Valusek

Production Manager: Dave Conant
Photo Researcher: Marjorie Benson
Photo Reserarch Assistant:
Terri Willis

Printed on Evergreen Gloss
50% recycled preconsumer waste
Binder's board made from 100% recycled material

Library of Congress Cataloging-in-Publication Data

Challand, Helen J.
    Disappearing wetlands / Helen J. Challand.
       p. cm. -- (Saving planet earth)
    Includes index.
    Summary: Examines the ecological role of wetlands and discusses how they
are formed, what life they support, and how people modify or destroy them.
    ISBN 0-516-05511-9
    1. Wetlands--Juvenile literature. 2. Wetland conservation--Juvenile literature.
3. Wetlands--North America--Juvenile literature. [1. Wetland ecology. 2. Ecology.]
I. Title. II. Series.
QH87.3.C43 1992
333.91'816--dc20

                                                 91-38243
                                                    CIP
                                                        AC

Cover photo—© Imtek Imagineering/Masterfile

TABLE OF CONTENTS

Chapter 1

Buried in the Bog

A HEAVY MIST HUNG over the English countryside. It seemed to rise out of the thick plant growth that choked the ground. Andy Mould and Eddie Slack had come to Lindow Moss to cut peat to sell as fuel. The two men had worked there before, but this day in August 1984 would be different.

Over 10,000 years ago, the peat bog known as Lindow Moss in Cheshire, England, was the site of a 1,500-acre (607-hectare) lake. For centuries, the spongy plant called sphagnum moss and other plants died and fell into the lake, which had little oxygen in it. As the lake filled in, the plants failed to decompose completely. Instead, more and more of them piled on top, and they gradually changed into a rich, moist dark-brown mass called peat. If left alone and covered with rock over many more millions of years, peat would have turned into coal. But the peat wasn't covered, and it hasn't been left alone. Humans discovered long ago that peat can be cut into blocks, dried, and used as fuel.

Suddenly as their huge excavating machine cut deeper, Andy and Eddie saw something that made them quickly cut the power. A human foot was sticking out of the peat.

Work stopped immediately and the authorities were called. The rest of the body must be there somewhere.

Once the police discovered that the foot and leg did not belong to someone recently buried, an archeologist, a scientist who studies ancient civilizations, was called in. Soon other scientists arrived. To prevent any more damage to the ancient body, they used only their hands to uncover the other parts of the corpse.

The ancient man had a cord wrapped around his neck, as if he had been murdered or executed. The browned flesh

Lindow Man, the murdered man found in a British bog. Lindow Man now resides in the British Museum.

glistened as acid bog water dripped from it. The skin and muscles were shriveled, but they were still attached to the skeleton, which was soft and mushy.

Very carefully, the well-preserved body was transported to a laboratory in London. There, the scientists determined that Lindow Man, as they called him, lived about 300 B.C. They learned how tall he was, what he ate for his last meal, and how he may have died. They even know his blood type (O) and the fact that his short hair was intentionally cut.

FACT

Some 2,000 bodies of ancient people have been found in the wetland bogs of Europe. Archeologists have dated them from 800 B.C. to A.D. 400. So far, the bogs of Germany have yielded the most—215. Denmark has produced 166; Britain and Ireland, 120; and Holland, 48.

In 1982, construction workers uncovered some human skulls in a Florida bog. They turned out to belong to some early American Indians buried some 7,000 to 8,000 years ago. The skulls contained shrunken brain tissue. The scientists could retrieve some DNA, the genetic material in cells that determines the characteristics we will have. The oldest DNA ever collected, it may help us learn about early man.

Why are Lindow Man and the others like him important? Most of what we know about ancient people has been learned from their bones, because their flesh has long since decomposed. But the special qualities of the wetlands we know as bogs have the ability to preserve human flesh. Thus we can learn more about people who lived long ago.

Scientific interest in bog bodies has been great. But for the most part, people ignored the bogs themselves. Now, however, we're discovering that it's also important to understand the bogs and similar wetland areas around the world. They play a vital role in the environment and natural resources of the whole planet.

Wetlands Are Not Wastelands

Wetlands are places where water and land meet. But not all such places are wetlands. A depression in a farmyard where water sits for days after it rains is probably not a wetland. To be a wetland, an area must have special characteristics, which are described in the next chapter.

There are many different types of wetlands, each with its own unique characteristics. A bog such as Lindow Moss is one kind. Others include marshes, swamps, estuaries, bays, and deltas. And sometimes, just to make matters more confusing, the same word is used for quite different types of wetlands in different parts of North America. Wetlands can

Treeless wetlands called marshes are home to many kinds of waterfowl such as this family of Canada geese.

9

be both inland, where they contain fresh water, and along seacoasts, where they contain salt water.

We will be looking closely at some of these valuable natural resources—how they were formed, which animals live in and around them, and the role people play in modifying (changing) or destroying them.

Many wetlands such as this one in Michigan have been treated as outdoor garbage dumps. Most people did not know they were endangering other living things by using wetlands as wastelands.

For centuries, wetland areas were considered useless. These wet, soggy lands were regarded as wastelands and nuisances. They often smell like rotten eggs, so people assumed that it was all right to use them as dumping grounds for all kinds of wastes.

People drained the water from wetland areas or filled them in so that they could be used for housing developments. They were filled in for farmland and highways and dredged for shipping channels. This draining and filling was called land reclamation because the land was being "reclaimed" for human use instead of being left to mosquitoes. Destruction of wetlands was considered progress.

Only recently have we become aware that wetlands are truly wild and wondrous communities. In their natural state, they provide breeding grounds for millions of birds and other water animals, many of them endangered. Wetlands can prevent flooding rivers and lakes from reaching homes and businesses. They lessen erosion of the soil, add to the supply of fresh water found underground, filter out sediment, and absorb pollutants. In addition, they provide beautiful, tranquil areas for recreation and pleasure.

Farmers, developers, scientists and environmentalists continue to argue over the definition of a wetland. Is every long-lasting mud puddle a wetland? Is an area that is only occasionally wet a wetland?

As the argument goes on, time is running out as fast as the water is drained out of wetlands. We must act now to understand the value of what we have and save what is left before it is destroyed beyond repair.

The meandering Alatna River in Alaska flows from the North Brooks Range. Untouched wetlands lie between the huge curves the river has taken across the landscape.

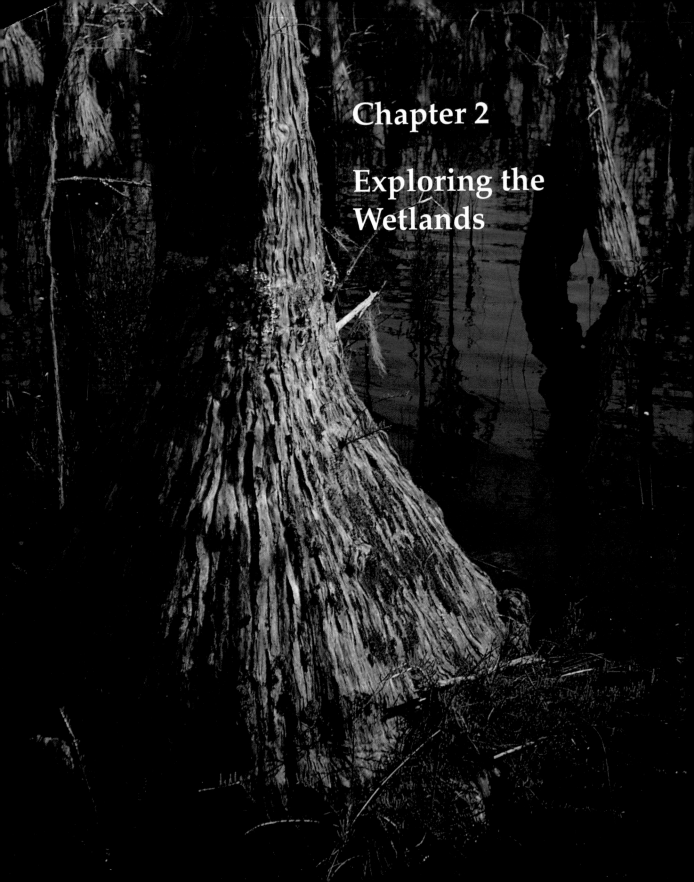

Chapter 2

Exploring the Wetlands

HAVE YOU EVER WATCHED a flock of ducks or geese flying overhead? You hear their loud calls as the birds signal to each other. Perhaps you're lucky enough to live in an area where millions of birds fly over during the spring or fall. That means that you live on a regular route that migrating birds often fly, a path called a flyway. If that's the case, you probably already know that waterfowl often follow rivers and cross lakes and wetlands where they will find plenty of food on their rest stops.

Wetlands are found in most areas of the world. They occur wherever low-lying land meets water or rivers meet oceans. Some of the most productive and interesting habitats on Earth occur in these "in-between" places. Thousands of species call wetlands home—or at least a nice place to visit.

Wetlands are areas where land (terrestrial habitat) gradually becomes water (aquatic, or deep-water, habitat). The kinds of plants and animals that inhabit a wetland vary depending on how wet or how dry a specific area is. The dry area elevated above a wet area is called an upland. The plants and animals that live in the upland may be quite different from those in the wetland. And the ones that inhabit the area where the two meet may be different yet.

This wetland is located where Wisconsin's Mink River empties into Lake Michigan.

13

Defining a Wetland

It isn't easy to define a wetland because for every description you can find, you can also find exceptions. However, the U.S. Fish and Wildlife Service has developed a definition of wetland that is in use around the world. According to that government agency, wetland is land that meets three characteristics.

One, it is covered by water or has waterlogged soil during the growing season. Waterlogged soil is saturated soil—it contains so much water that oxygen is driven out of it.

Two, the soil is *hydric soil*, which means that it has characteristics that developed in the absence of oxygen. Most soil contains plenty of oxygen for plant roots to take what they need. But hydric soil is mostly *anaerobic*, which means that it does not have enough oxygen for upland plants to grow. You can't always tell by looking at soil if it is hydric; usually only a soil scientist can tell.

However, you can identify many wetlands by the third characteristic. Wetlands usually have growing in them special kinds of plants called hydrophytes. These are plants that are specially adapted to growing in hydric soils. Cattails and sawgrass are familiar hydrophytes. They have evolved the ability to survive with less soil oxygen than other plants need. Hydrophytes have the special ability to take oxygen from the air or water in various ways and send it to their foliage.

Unfortunately, many areas do not have all three characteristics and are still wetlands. Also, the descriptions of the characteristics may vary. For example, there is a lot of

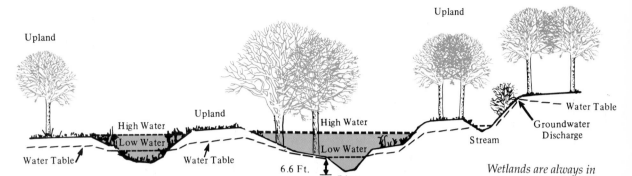

Wetlands are always in a state of change as the water table rises and falls.

discussion going on currently about just how much and when water needs to be there for an area to be a wetland. There is further debate about whether an area has to have all three characteristics to be included as a wetland. This doesn't sound very important, but it can be vital to a person who owns land.

This all sounds as if wetlands are not very good places for living things. But far from being "waste" places, wetlands are the most productive habitats on Earth. That means they grow more plants and animal life in equal areas per year than any other habitat, even tropical rain forests.

Although cattails are one of the most common hydrophytes, they aren't the most beautiful. Flowering hydrophytes, such as this wild marsh iris, make wetlands colorful wonderlands.

Types of Wetlands

No two wetlands are alike. Some are the size of a wading pool and others are huge, such as the Everglades in Florida, which is 4,000 square miles (10,360 square kilometers). Some wetland areas stay wet all year, while others are very dry except perhaps for one season of the year. Still other areas may be dry for years but come to life as water returns.

The shape and size of any particular wetland area are usually determined by the kinds of plants, the hydrophytes, that live there. In fact, a wetland may change in size or shape year after year as the amount of water that reaches it varies. Surprisingly, a wetland can even be on the side of a hill if there is a patch of soil on that hillside that collects and holds water as it runs out of the hill. Marsh marigold, sundews, water hemlock, skunk cabbage, cattail, and blue flag are some common hydrophytes.

Because wetlands appear to be so different, they have been given a variety of names—swamp, bog, fen, pocosin, marsh, estuary, floodplain, pothole, mudflat, lagoon, bay, playa, slough, sinkhole, tundra, and bayou.

And because there are so many common names given to different wetland areas—names that don't necessarily mean the same thing to different people—scientists are now grouping wetlands according to a different pattern. They call the wetlands that are marsh-like *palustrine.* That name, in fact, means "marshy." Marshes, bogs, and swamps are palustrine wetlands. Those wetlands that have deeper water are called *lacustrine,* which means lake-like. Marshes and swamps where the water is salty but not as salty as the ocean are called *estuarine.* These *brackish* (salty) wetlands are usually along seacoasts.

Potters Marsh is only ten miles south of downtown Anchorage, Alaska. City dwellers call it their "urban wildlife marsh." Alaska has more untouched wetlands than any other state.

Two others terms are also used: *riverine,* meaning in rivers, and *marine,* meaning out in the salty ocean and along beaches. However, rivers and oceans are two very big topics on their own and they are not being covered in this book.

To simplify the different wetlands, we will group them according to whether they are inland (containing fresh water) or coastal (containing salt water).

Inland Wetlands

Inland wetlands, the kind most of us are familiar with, may be wet temporarily (30 days or less), seasonally (6 months or less), or permanently (year-round). Georgia's Okefenokee Swamp is a famous inland wetland.

Some of the most common inland wetlands were formed about 10,000 years ago when the glaciers and huge seas that once covered much of North America began to shrink. As they shrank, they left pockets, or depressions, in the land. These pockets soon filled with water.

But wetlands are not always ancient. Even today natural events and people can make wetlands appear or disappear.

Wind makes wetland areas by eroding, or carrying away, loose soil and sand little by little, leaving depressions that are filled by rain or by runoff from the surrounding land. Some wetlands are found in uplands; others are deep enough to reach down into the water table—the top of the water that lies underground.

Volcanoes, landslides, and the movement of the gigantic plates in the Earth's crust can also change the shape of the land, leaving holes or depressions that turn into wetlands.

Even animals can make wetlands. When beavers dam a river or stream, the water has nowhere to go except out onto the land around the river, turning meadows into marshes and forested areas into swamps.

Finally, humans can make wetlands. We build dikes and dams to hold water where there was none before. We mine minerals, leaving huge holes that fill with water.

No matter how the hole forms, if it fills with water, it will soon begin to grow water plants because the seeds of some wetland plants, like cattails and willows, are easily carried by the air.

Although inland wetlands are formed in different ways, marshes, swamps, and bogs are the most common types of the palustrine wetlands.

Freshwater Marshes

A common freshwater marsh is a wetland that is dominated by herbaceous (nonwoody) plants such as grasses. No shrubs or trees live in a marsh, though they often grow on the upland around it. Marshes are usually formed along rivers or in water-filled depressions in the earth.

The water in a marsh may not even be visible when you stand near it. Or it might be up to 7 feet (2.1 meters) deep, such as along the edges of a deep lake. These shallow waters heat up during the day and cool at night. Marsh life must adjust to these changing temperatures.

During daylight, marsh plants use large amounts of carbon dioxide to make food. In this process, called *photosynthesis*, they release oxygen. At night, plants take in oxygen and release carbon dioxide.

Cattails, sedges, rushes, and arrowhead are common marsh plants that anchor themselves in the marsh mud with tough roots or thickened underground stems called rhizomes that send out new shoots. These plants prefer standing in water with their "heads" high in the air. Other rooted plants, like the water lilies on page 42, may send their leaves to the surface to trap sunlight.

Aquatic plants such as elodea and pondweed stay at or below the surface. Duckweed, the smallest flowering plant, simply floats on the surface with its roots in the water. Algae, the simplest green plants, often reproduce so fast that they form a carpet of green scum on open water. Marsh marigold, lobelia, and iris grow in the shallow marsh edges.

The large amount of vegetation growing in a marsh provides excellent habitat for a wide variety of wildlife. Even the algae "scum" on the surface of the water supports other life.

Marsh plants and animals can be beautiful and unusual. The fringed gentian (above) is an exquisite marsh flower. The capybara (right), the largest rodent in the world, is found in Venezuelan marshes.

A marsh teems with animal life. Crayfish, hydra, planaria, snails, and cyclops crawl or swim everywhere. Amphibians burrow in the soft ooze. Many of the 2,600 species of frogs live in marshes.

Mammals from the surrounding upland come down to drink or fish. Muskrats use cattails to construct mounds for their homes, similar to the homes of beavers. Raccoons, mink, deer, and busy rodents occupy the area surrounding the water, often wading into the water and feeding from it.

And then there are the birds. If you see a redwing blackbird, there is probably a marsh nearby. Grebes, marsh hawks, teals, coots, and rails are some waterbirds that use marshes for breeding and raising their young and as rest stops on their yearly migrations.

FACT

One study found almost 700 species of living things in a single wetland area. That included 489 species of plants, 126 kinds of birds, 32 species of fish, 21 varieties of mammals, and 12 kinds of reptiles. The U.S. Fish and Wildlife Service lists 104 marsh-living plants and animals as endangered.

Long-billed curlews (above) migrate over inland wetlands from the Arctic to Mexico. Their numbers have decreased because of the loss of wetland breeding grounds to agriculture. Pickerel weed (right) grows in shallow marsh waters. Muskrats and wood ducks eat pickerel seeds for food. April flowers of marsh marigold (left) signal the beginning of spring in many freshwater wetlands. Birds begin nesting and fish move into the marshes to spawn.

Freshwater Marsh

Common Cattails

wing blackbird

Wood ducks

Water lilies

Arrowhead

Sora Rail

Dissolved Oxygen in Marshes

Using a water-testing kit from a plumbing store or your local natural resources office, you can check the health of various bodies of water in your community.

Aquatic life needs the right amounts of oxygen, carbon dioxide, and pH conditions, in addition to food, of course. Each of these factors can be determined with the test kit.

One reading you will get is for DO, meaning dissolved oxygen. Oxygen is dissolved in water, meaning it is completely part of the water, not separate bubbles. Factors that affect the DO reading include seasonal changes, temperature, amount of sunlight, depth in the water, wind, and water currents.

The carbon dioxide reading depends upon the number of green plants present and the amount of decomposition, as well as physical variations in the environment.

Select several bodies of water to test and compare. These might be a swamp, a slow farmland stream, a fast-flowing river, and a marsh. Test your sites twice a year for several years, preferably in spring and early fall when the water depth will vary quite a bit. If this study is done as a school project, the teacher can keep the records and help each incoming class draw comparisons.

Bogs—Places of Mystery

In 1919, British aviators John Alcock and Arthur Whitten Brown made the first nonstop flight across the Atlantic Ocean from Newfoundland to Ireland. When they reached Ireland, they saw a smooth, green surface in a perfect place to land. Their wheels touched down . . . and down, until the nose of their fragile plane sank into the trembling ground beneath them. They had landed in a bog.

As Lindow Man knew, bogs are places that seem different from the rest of the land, perhaps even mysterious places. Things that go into bogs often never come out.

Sphagnum moss, one of the main mosses in bogs. Most bogs lie in the Northern Hemisphere where they formed in kettle holes, depressions left by receding glaciers.

Bogs are wetlands that have no source of water but rainfall and consist primarily of mosses. The water chemistry of a bog is quite different from that of other marshes. Because there is no water flow, there is little dissolved oxygen in the water, so conditions are anaerobic— without oxygen. And because the mosses make the water acidic, not many bacteria can live. Therefore, when plants die and fall into the water, they are not decomposed by bacteria and fungi as dead things usually are. Instead, they pile up and are compressed over the centuries. The plant matter that forms is peat, which accumulates in bogs at the rate of several inches every hundred years.

Effect of Acid on Bone

An Earth Experience

Cook a chicken or turkey thigh until the meat falls away from the bone. Clean off every piece of muscle, gristle, and fat.

Place the bone in a glass jar and cover it with vinegar. Vinegar is an acid with a pH of about 3.5. That is over 1,000 times more acidic than distilled water. Cap the jar and set it aside. After about two weeks, remove the bone from the vinegar. How does it feel? Try to break the bone.

Some bog plants, like these pitcher plants, are insectivorous. They trap and digest insects. Some scientists believe that Venus's flytrap and other such plants evolved to eat insects in order to obtain the nutrients that the bog lacks.

Because of the acidic and anaerobic conditions, a bog has fewer species of living things than other wetlands. But the plants and animals that call a bog their home are unique.

Trees that grow in a bog include poison oak, tamarack,

An Earth Experience

Growing Insect-Eating Plants

The pitcher plant, sundew, and Venus's flytrap are three kinds of plants found in bogs or swamps. Their oddly shaped leaves have devices that allow them to trap insects. They secrete an enzyme that digests the protein in them.

These special plants may be purchased from most scientific supply houses or perhaps from a local plant store. Do not collect them from nature. There are few left in the wild.

Prepare a terrarium before you buy your plants. They need a glass box with a top that holds in the moisture. These plants cannot stand dry air. Cover the bottom of the terrarium with coarse gravel to allow for drainage. Mix 2 parts garden soil with 1 part peat moss. This will provide the acid soil that insect-eating plants love.

After you've seeded the plant in the soil, add a layer of sphagnum moss to the top of the soil and around the plants. Water the

Many bogs, both natural and artificial, are used to grow cranberries for canning, freezing, and sale as fresh berries.

leatherleaf, and buckbean. Berry bushes are plentiful—cranberry, partridge, bunch, and blueberry.

Since the water in a bog is often acidic, few, if any, fish live there. Some amphibians and reptiles, such as the

soil well, and cover the terrarium. Place it near a window but not in direct sunlight.

Try to catch flies, ants, and gnats by placing an open jar outdoors with a little sugar water or syrup rubbed on the bottom and sides inside the jar. When several insects have become trapped in the jar, cap it. At home, remove the cap and lay the jar inside the terrarium. Quickly replace the glass cover.

Sit back and watch what happens. Insectivorous plants enjoy digesting an insect now and then, but they do not depend on them for food. Like other green plants, these plants make their own food by photosynthesis.

endangered bog turtle, like this unusual habitat, however. Mammals that frequent bogs include the bog lemming, Canada lynx, otter, and mink. Birds, though limited, include juncos, kinglets, waxwings, warblers, owls, and hawks.

Peat Harvests. Half of the peat grounds in the world are in the Soviet Union. Canada is second. In the United States, which has only one-sixteenth of the world's peat, Florida harvests and sells the most of any state. The peat is chopped up as an ingredient in prepared soil used by greenhouses because it holds vast amounts of water. It also can be dried and burned as a fuel.

Peat has about half the fuel energy of coal. It is estimated that the state of Minnesota has about 7 million acres (2.8 million hectares) of peat. This energy source alone could meet the needs of all the people in the state for over 200 years. The Soviet Union has more than 70 power plants that burn peat to make electricity.

Ireland gets about 20 percent of its energy from peat. However, the bogs that are being harvested for their peat are irreplaceable. New peat is always being made but not at a fast enough rate to be of any use to us as an energy source.

Prairie Potholes

From the southern Canadian provinces of Alberta to Manitoba down to Montana, the Dakotas, Iowa, and Minnesota in the United States, rolling prairie land extends as far as the eye can see. When glaciers receded from these prairies, they left thousands of potholes—small, shallow depressions filled with water and vegetation. Potholes are a type of marsh, though they don't all contain fresh water. Some western states have very salty potholes.

About a third of potholes cover only 1 to 10 acres (0.4 to 4 hectares). The rest are larger. There may be as many as a hundred potholes per square mile (2.6 square kilometers), making some areas of the prairie look pockmarked.

The grassy uplands surrounding potholes provide nesting places for ducks and geese during breeding season. The groups of young, called broods, are then led to the potholes to feed. They also find safe cover from predators in the pothole vegetation. It is estimated that 7 million ducks nest and breed every year in the potholes of the

Some farmers realize that potholes are valuable to the environment and to wildlife. They preserve them by plowing around them.

Teal nests like this often are lost to predators in the grassy upland of a prairie pothole.

upper Midwest. Many species use potholes as food sources and rest stops during migrations. Other species, such as mallards, pintails, and curlews, spend their summers at potholes. Over half the waterfowl in North America use potholes at some time during the year.

Freshwater Swamps

Like marshes, swamps may be wet temporarily, seasonally, or permanently. Unlike marshes, swamps are dominated by woody plants, especially shrubs and trees with shallow root systems. They often spread horizontally along rivers where water floods after heavy storms or when winter snows melt.

The water in a swamp is usually shallow, rarely exceeding 3 feet (0.9 meter). The water temperature may vary as much as 30 degrees Fahrenheit (16.7 degrees Celsius) during the day.

Dissolved oxygen may be 8 to 10 parts per million (ppm) during the daylight hours and drop to less than 1 ppm at night when the plants are less active.

Streams flowing into swamps bring in quantities of nutrients. Decaying trees and the presence of mosses may darken the waters. A swamp may be acidic or alkaline (basic), depending on the kind of rock beneath it. An acidic swamp has different kinds of plants than an alkaline swamp.

One of the best-known swamps in North America is the Okefenokee, on the border of Georgia and Florida. It is famous for its water tupelo (also called swamp gum) and bald cypress trees. The bald cypress grows with special projections from the roots, called cypress knees, which help support the trees.

The water level in a bottomland swamp changes each season. These cypress and tupelo trees show that the water may reach almost 10 feet (3 meters) high during flooding.

Rivers and their Wetlands

The level of the water in rushing streams and rivers rises and falls. Heavy rainfalls and rapidly melting snow cause rivers to swell. When the banks can no longer contain the raging water, the river overflows onto the land. The churning water carries with it tons of sediment. As the water recedes and the sediment settles out of it, floodplains, also called bottomlands, are created.

Many freshwater swamps originally formed in the floodplains of rivers. Generally, however, floodplains are under water only part of the year, so quite different plants can grow on them than grow on lands that are always wet. The most obvious of these bottomland plants are hardwood trees. Abundant shrubbery and vines grow among the trees. Together they hold the fertile soil in place when the waters rush in and ebb out during flood seasons. Unfortunately, most of these bottomland hardwood forests around the world have been harvested.

Who owns the floodplains? They really belong to the river. However, people like living along a river. It provides them with a scenic view and an avenue for transportation. The floodplain has rich soil of silt and peat, which is ideal for agriculture.

All over the world humans have built towns and cities on these unpredictable lands. Industrial sites spring up along riverbanks. Recreational parks claim their share of floodplains. It sounds like a success story—man has tamed the wild rivers.

Not so. Preventing the river from reclaiming its own territory is a constant struggle.

The Kafue Flats in Zambia, Africa, is a broad floodplain of 5 million acres (2 million hectares) formed by the Kafue River, a tributary of the Zambezi. Every year these lands flood for several months. Wildlife in the area has adjusted to alternating periods of mud and flood.

But now two large dams have been built in the river to provide water for hydroelectric plants. The western side of the river is actually drying up, and shrubs and trees are taking over. The eastern side still gets flooded. The entire way of life of the animals is changing. The animal habitats began to change the minute the dams went in and are already lost. What will win out in the long run—the people's need for electric power or the environment?

Because floodplains have very rich soil, people want to own them and develop the land. This floodplain in Nova Scotia, Canada, will be protected by new laws that limit development.

Deltas. A delta can be regarded as a floodplain that forms at the mouth of a river. It is often shaped like a triangle. As fast-moving river currents near the ocean (or as two rivers meet to form a wider river), the waters slow down. They literally push against the standing waters they are meeting. This causes the water to spread out and drop the particles of soil it carries. The particles pile up as sediment, forming new wetland with rich, nutrient-filled soil.

Delta marshes can be fresh water, like the vast wetlands in southern Illinois that form where the Ohio River meets the Mississippi. Or they can be saline, such as where the Mississippi meets the Gulf of Mexico.

If a delta is left undisturbed, it grows each year. The delta of the Nile River in Egypt gains about 12 feet (3.7 meters) each year. The delta at the mouth of the Mississippi used to grow up to 200 feet (60.8 meters) a year. Towns built at the mouth of the river several hundred years ago are now far inland.

This man-made levee (the curve at the left side) was built to hold back the flood waters of the Mississippi River. The area to the right of the road was once wetland.

The Nile Delta as seen from a space shuttle. Cairo is located where the river forms the delta.

Forming a Delta

*Construct a "river" by nailing 1-inch (2.5-centimeter) strips of
wood vertically down the sides of a board at least 2 feet (61 centimeters) long. Use waterproof tape along the sides where they
join the bottom.*

*Place a block of wood 2 inches (5 centimeters) square at
the "headwaters" or upper end of the trough. The lower end
or "mouth" of the trough should be placed on the edge of a
large cake pan. Put a layer of stones, gravel, sand, silt, and
clay all along the bottom of the trough.*

*Fill a pitcher with water and pour it slowly into the
raised end. As the water heads for the "sea," it will carry
material with it. What shape does the water take as it
leaves the mouth of the river? Which material falls first?
What happens to the silt and clay? It takes time and lots
of sediments to form a delta.*

In Canada, the Athabasca and Peace Rivers in northern
Alberta form deltas side by side. The wetland area formed
by these deltas covers 1.5 million acres (607,000 hectares). It
is wild country full of all types of North American wildlife.
Enormous bison, perhaps 5,000 of them, roam the meadows
around the wetlands of Wood Buffalo National Park. Muskrats and beavers dam streams, changing the landscape.

All four major North American flyways (the main paths
birds take when they are migrating) cross the delta area.
Summer and fall visitors to these deltas include millions of
birds, such as snow geese, swans, and piping plovers. Many

species stay long enough to raise young.

Since 1968, when Bennett Dam was built on the Peace River, the delta has been drying out, affecting all of that wonderful wildlife. In the 1970s, weirs (partial dams) were built on some of the outflowing rivers to raise the delta's water level and repair some of the damage.

Coastal Wetlands

Along seacoasts, weather conditions, seasons, and tides bring constant change. Sediment from rivers and debris deposited by ocean currents form several types of coastal wetlands—saltwater marshes and swamps, estuaries, mudflats, lagoons, coastal bays, and sloughs.

Coastal wetlands contain salt water or, if they are in areas where freshwater rivers and saltwater tides meet, *brackish* water, which is part salty and part fresh. The kinds of plants and animals that can live in such water are usually quite different from those in freshwater wetlands.

Estuaries. Many rivers and streams on the continents eventually run into the ocean. An estuary is where the fresh

The Athabasca Delta (left) in northern Alberta, Canada, is part of one of the largest freshwater delta systems in the world. Flocks of snow geese (right) live in the delta during certain seasons of the year.

water mixes with salt water. An estuary is one of the most productive communities on Earth. It has more life and more varieties of life than most other places.

The salinity of an estuary varies with the time of year. During hot, dry months, there is less fresh water coming down the river, so more salt water moves in. Melting snow and spring rains bring more fresh water into the estuary.

The depth of the salt water varies with the tides and winds. Saltier water is heavy and sinks to the bottom, while fresh water stays on the surface. Currents and winds spread salt through all levels.

Estuaries are high in dissolved oxygen and nutrients because of the water coming in from the sea and out from the rivers. Estuaries teem with life because they have plenty of food to go around.

An estuary is often called the "cradle of the ocean." It is the nursery for millions of saltwater fish and shellfish. Two-thirds of all such animals use estuaries at some time during

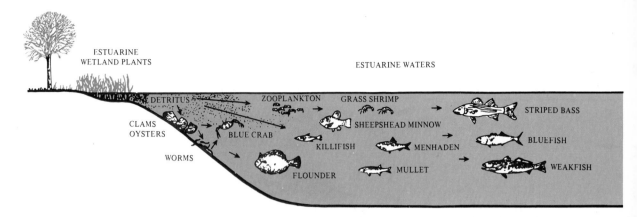

ESTUARINE
WETLAND PLANTS

ESTUARINE WATERS

DETRITUS
ZOOPLANKTON
GRASS SHRIMP
STRIPED BASS

CLAMS
OYSTERS
SHEEPSHEAD MINNOW

BLUE CRAB
KILLIFISH
MENHADEN
BLUEFISH

WORMS
FLOUNDER
MULLET
WEAKFISH

their lives. Adults come in to spawn, or lay their eggs. The young fish, called fry, stay in the estuary until they are large enough to escape danger in open waters. They will return to these same grounds to start another generation.

Because of sediments deposited as river waters slow down, an estuary often consists of large areas called mudflats, which fill with water during high tide. As the tide falls, it leaves nutritious sediments behind that are used by numerous invertebrates. During low tide, the water drains out, leaving the flats exposed. Low tide is a time when people often regard mudflats as smelly. Invertebrate animals become invisible as they burrow into the mud. Many tube worms and mollusks such as clams and snails live in mudflats. So, too, do the crustaceans such as crabs.

Between the mudflats and open water may be vast beds of eelgrass or other sea grasses. They trap the nutrients. They also decompose, adding to

The food chain spreading out from an estuary, showing how commercially important fish depend on this wetland

Shrimp are among the crustaceans that live in estuaries during part of their life cycle.

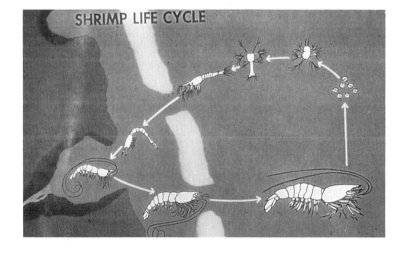

SHRIMP LIFE CYCLE

 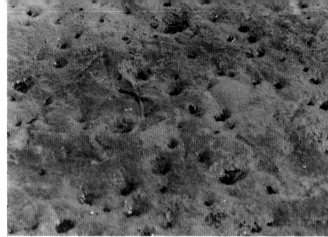

When the water drains out of an estuary during low tide, mudflats (left) are exposed to the air. All kinds of small animals burrow down below the surface, creating numerous small pits (right).

the organic material in the water, which is called detritus. It supports huge numbers of microscopic living things which, in turn, serve as food for estuary animals.

An estuary is home to all types of migrating and resident birds. Cormorants and pelicans dine on the abundant fish. Egrets, herons, and bitterns walk through the shallow waters to feast upon aquatic life. Hawks and bald eagles dive from the air when their keen eyesight sees fish near the surface.

Saltwater Marshes. Saltwater marshes are also called tidal marshes. They form in estuaries, on offshore sandbars, on islands, and on spits—narrow points of land jutting out into the water.

The plant life in a saltwater marsh is unique. Twice a day as the tides come in the vegetation is bathed by salt water.

Grasses and other herbaceous plants dominate saltwater marshes. They include eelgrass, pickleweed, saltmarsh cordgrass, saltgrass, and other plants that have adapted to life in salt water. Pickleweed, for example, has developed special cells that hold water. When salt water is taken in, the excess water held in the cells dilutes, or weakens, the salinity. Saltgrass has special cells that gather salt and excrete it through openings on the underside of their leaves. Thus only fresh water gets inside the plant.

Estuaries: Where rivers meet oceans

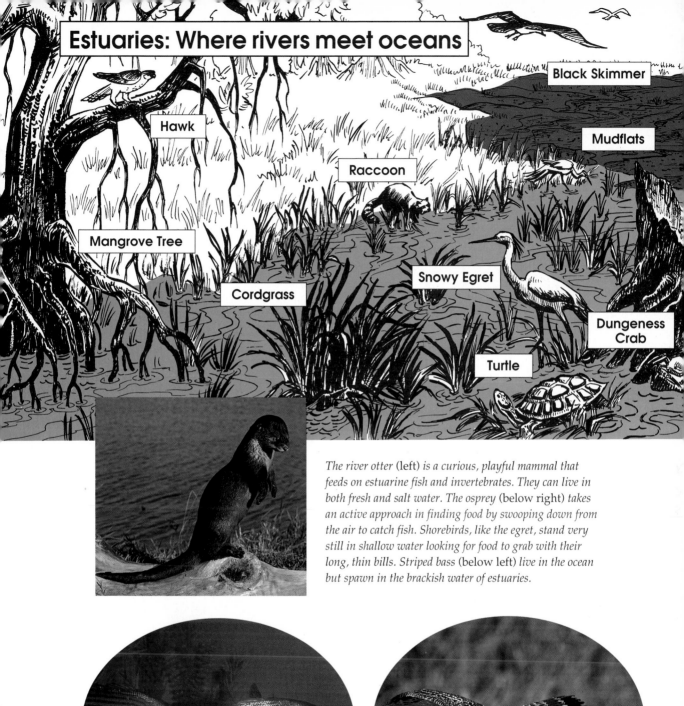

Black Skimmer

Mudflats

Hawk

Raccoon

Mangrove Tree

Snowy Egret

Cordgrass

Dungeness Crab

Turtle

The river otter (left) is a curious, playful mammal that feeds on estuarine fish and invertebrates. They can live in both fresh and salt water. The osprey (below right) takes an active approach in finding food by swooping down from the air to catch fish. Shorebirds, like the egret, stand very still in shallow water looking for food to grab with their long, thin bills. Striped bass (below left) live in the ocean but spawn in the brackish water of estuaries.

Saltwater marshes may develop along shores that are protected from waves by sandy coastal islands called barrier islands. Sapelo Island, Georgia (above), contains 3,811 acres (1,542 hectares) of saltwater marshes. Pickleweed (left) has adapted to the salt in such marshes.

The food supply for wildlife is plentiful in a saltwater marsh. Nutrients are brought into it from both the ocean and the rivers. Blue-green algae thrive in these wetlands. They have the wonderful ability to take free nitrogen from the air (something that most plants can't do) and change it to the nitrates that higher green plants can use in making proteins for growth and energy.

FACT

One acre (0.4 hectare) of saltwater marsh produces about 10 tons (9 metric tons) of food per year for animals. A farmer's hay field, on the other hand, produces only about 4 tons (3.6 metric tons) and takes up lots more room.

Fish, such as silversides, stickleback, flounder, and blue-fish, thrive in the brackish waters of coastal marshes. Most of them are predators that feed on smaller fish, insects, and other aquatic animals. The fiddler crab, ribbed mussel, periwinkle, oyster, and marsh snail are found in the brackish water.

Herons, blackbirds, curlews, brown pelicans, bald eagles, and golden plovers find plenty of fish and invertebrates. Twice a day, the tide brings in a feast for everyone.

The Ballona wetland is a salt marsh that is now located in the heart of Los Angeles, California. Occupying only 153 acres (61.9 hectares), it is visited by 129 bird species, including the endangered least tern, 25 species of fish, 29 species of mammals, and 9 species of reptiles and amphibians.

FACT

Saltwater Swamps. Coastal swamps are very like tropical rain forests, with large trees and jungly growth. The tides and amount of salt determine the kinds of plants and animals that use this type of wetland.

Most tropical saltwater swamps around the world are dominated by specialized trees called mangroves. Not many trees can stand in salt water—let alone absorb it and live. The sap in some species of mangrove is ten times saltier than

Red mangrove trees are held in the shallow swamp mud by aerial or prop roots. These roots stabilize the trees and send oxygen to regular roots below the surface.

39

These scientists are using a gill net to gather samples of plant and animal life in a mangrove swamp. They will study the samples to check on the health and productivity of the mangrove system.

the sap of a maple tree. Some species actually secrete salt out of their leaves.

Once 60 percent of the Earth's tropical shores were covered with mangrove swamps. A little over half of them remain today. Each year, 3,000 to 4,000 square miles (7,700 to 10,360 square kilometers) are destroyed.

Mangrove trees have aerial roots that hold them in the gooey mud, which is too shallow for regular tree roots. Prop roots grow out and down from the trunk and branches. They carry oxygen down to the regular roots under water.

A mangrove swamp is twenty times more productive than open ocean. Since mangroves are evergreen they never get completely bare, but they drop some leaves every day so the waters get a constant new supply of nutrients for the abundant life that surrounds the trees.

As with freshwater swamps, thousands of animals either live in the salt swamp or come here to breed or just feed and rest before moving on. The fish, shrimp, and crab businesses depend heavily upon mangrove swamps for their supply of living produce. The water around the multitude of roots is teeming with life.

Parrots and egrets sit in the trees with monkeys, watching ibises, spoonbills, and herons walking in water looking for their supper. In Australia, water buffaloes look for food among the prop roots. The Bengal tigers roam around the mangroves in Bangladesh and India. The American crocodile—an endangered species—lives in mangroves along the tip of Florida.

The ABCs of Wetlands

Bay. Ocean inlet that is smaller than a gulf. Open, deeper water of an estuary with little wave action. Salt marshes form along its edges.

Bayou. Narrow, marshy strip of water flowing into or out of a lake or river. In the southeastern United States, a slow-moving stream meandering through bottomlands, swamps, and deltas.

Bog. Wetland of partially, decomposed layered plant material (usually sphagnum moss) called peat. Waterlogged, often acidic, and low in oxygen. Common in northern latitudes. Also called **peatland, pocosin, moor,** and **mire.**

> **Blanket bog**. Large peat deposits that "blanket" once-dry areas. Common in the United Kingdom.
>
> **Palsa bog**. Large, flat area of raised peat on the Arctic tundra.
>
> **Quaking bog**. A mat of peat moss or organic material floating on water. Spongy and bouncy to walk on.
>
> **Raised bog**. Dome-shaped bog raised above the ground. Called a high moor in Ireland.

Bottomland swamp. Seasonally flooded forested land next to rivers or lakes. Also called **bottomland hardwood forest, riparian/riverine wetland, swamp forest,** and **bosque.**

Delta. Flat area of sediment deposited at the mouth of a river, usually in a triangular shape.

Estuary. Wetland at the mouth of a river where it meets the ocean. Because of daily ocean tides, the water is very salty to brackish. Unvegetated areas exposed when the tide goes out are **mudflats.**

Fen. Waterlogged wetland fed by surface water or groundwater springs. Dominated by plants called sedges. Less acidic than bogs. Also called **mire, moor,** or **marsh** in Britain.

Floodplain. Seasonally flooded flat land along rivers or lakes.

Lagoon. Shallow pool or pond separated from open ocean by sand dunes, reefs, or soil banks.

Mangrove swamp. Coastal, saltwater wetland located in tropical or subtropical regions. Dominated by mangrove trees.

Marsh. Shallow, unforested wetland dominated by nonwoody plants such as grasses and cattails. Can be seasonally or permanently wet. Inland marshes contain fresh water; coastal marshes contain more salty water. **Ponds, potholes, sinkholes, wet prairies, wet meadows,** and **playas** are all types of marshy wetlands.

Playa. Shallow, circular basin filled by seasonal rains. Found in the southern plains of the United States.

Prairie pothole. Seasonally wet glacial depression or basin found in the northern prairies of the United States and Canada.

Shrub swamp. Waterlogged, freshwater wetland dominated by small trees and shrubs. Also called a **carr, shallow-water swamp,** or **thicket.**

Slough (pronounced *slew*). Common name for a swampy or marshy area. Can be a river inlet, a muddy creek, or an arm of an estuary.

Swamp. Forested wetland dominated by trees or shrubs. Swamps can be seasonally or permanently wet. Inland swamps contain fresh water; coastal swamps contain salt water. Also called **tree swamp, deep-water swamp,** or **bottomland.**

Tidal pool. Nutrient-rich shallow basin of water retained at low tide.

Wet meadow. Grassy open area where the soil is waterlogged within a few inches of the surface. No standing water during the growing season. Also called a **wet prairie.**

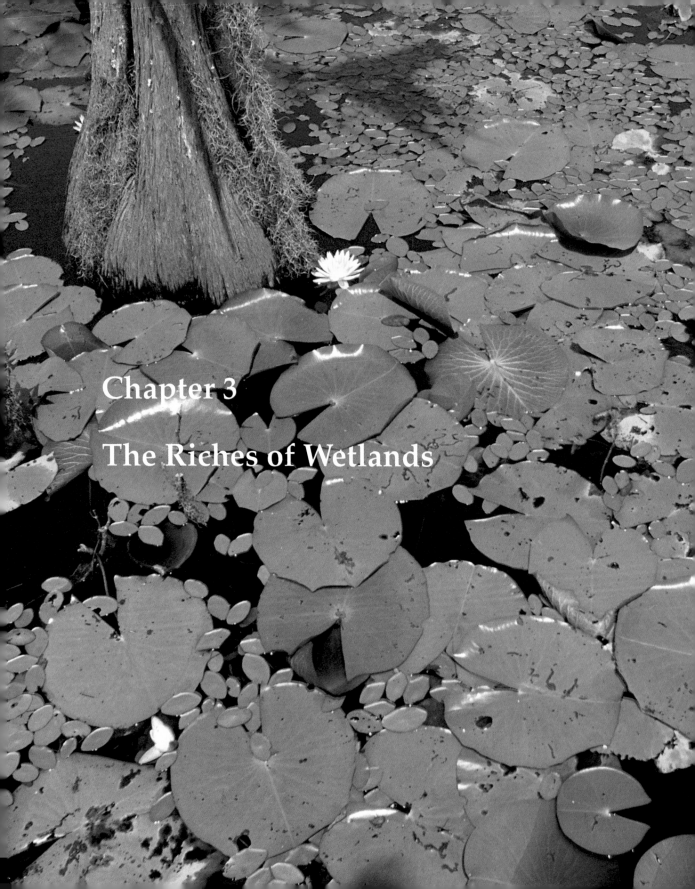

Chapter 3

The Riches of Wetlands

WETLANDS WERE ONCE looked upon as useless, infested waterholes. Some wetlands were valuable economically—they contained fuel (peat or coal), timber (bottomland hardwoods), or minerals. Otherwise, wetlands simply took up space that most people thought could be put to better use.

The value of a wetland was based only on the amount of money its products could bring. And, of course, once the desired product had been taken, the wetland was completely worthless.

Only recently has the public become aware of the importance of wetlands beyond their commercial possibilities. We are beginning to see that wetlands themselves are important natural resources.

Everyone pays for wetland destruction in a direct way. If wetlands are lost, more money is needed to build expensive wastewater treatment plants and flood-control projects. If plants and animals are lost, it means the loss of food for man, income for families, the possibility of using certain plants for medicine, and recreational activities. The benefits of healthy wetlands give us good reasons to conserve them for future generations.

The U.S. Army Corps of Engineers purchased wetland along the Charles River in Massachusetts because of its ability to control floods. They figure that if the wetlands had been drained and they had built flood-control structures instead, the cost to the residents for damage done by the flooding river would have been $17 million higher per year than it is.

FACT

Wetlands as Wildlife Habitat

When we think of wetlands we think first of ducks and other waterfowl. In fact, one of the first steps that the federal government took concerning wetlands was to create federal duck stamps. Hunters are required to buy stamps each fall to hunt ducks. The stamps are beautiful works of art that have become so popular many people who don't hunt buy the stamps just to collect them. Money from the sale of the stamps goes for the purchase of wetlands.

Ducks are good indicators of the general health of a wetland. If the ducks leave an area, it has probably been disturbed in some way.

Dabbling ducks, such as mallards, can start families in spring anywhere the females find an appropriate spot. And wetlands have many such spots. Dabbling ducks tip themselves forward in the water to reach underwater plants or invertebrates. Unlike diving ducks, they don't need deep water, so shallow wetlands are home. Diving ducks use wetlands, too, but they can go out into deep water to feed.

The mother duck generally wants about 1 foot (0.3 meter) of water where lots of reeds or cattails grow. Some grassy raised land nearby provides a good spot for laying her eggs and nesting. She lines the nest with grasses and sometimes with down from her own breast. After the ducklings hatch, they feed on the invertebrates and eventually on succulent water plants. The ducklings venture out of their nest for their first swim in the nearby water. When they are six to nine weeks old, they may be ready to fly.

Stopover for Migrants. Too often people are mainly concerned about the wetlands at either end of the birds' migratory trip. These are breeding and wintering grounds for many birds. There the birds build nests and the young are hatched. But birds need more than a summer home in Canada and a winter home in Louisiana or Texas. The wetlands between serve as "bed and breakfast" places during the long migration. You can't drive 3,000 miles (4,800 kilometers) across the continent without making several "pit stops." You need to sleep, go to the bathroom, and fuel up.

Dabbling ducks such as mallards thrive in wetlands. They gather food by tipping their bodies forward into the water (left). Uplands provide ducks with materials for building nests (right) and cover from enemies.

The same is true for millions of birds that fly north for the summer and south for the winter. They need large quantities of food to fatten up their small bodies for the flight.

More than 50 percent of the 800 or more species of protected migratory birds stop at wetlands.

America's tallest bird, the whooping crane, which was down to a count of 13 adults and 2 young in 1941, has been

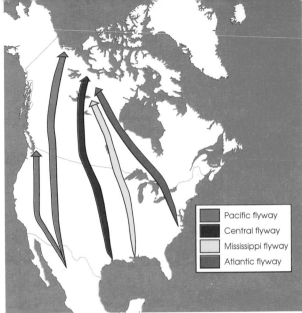

Pacific flyway
Central flyway
Mississippi flyway
Atlantic flyway

By 1990, the whooping crane population had risen to well over 100 birds in the wild, plus others that have been bred in captivity (above). Cranes are among the many birds that fly north in Canada along the four main cross-country routes called flyways (right).

rescued from extinction only because certain wetland areas have been dedicated to them. Whooping cranes spend the winter in the south, especially in the Aransas National Wildlife Refuge in Texas. They migrate north in spring and spend their breeding season and summer in northwest Canada.

As more and more land is turned over to agriculture, the duck population suffers. Since 1975 the number of geese and ducks in Canada and the United States has been reduced over 30 percent. The number of northern pintails, for example, dropped 75 percent in three decades. Mallards have not done much better. Their numbers are down 50 percent.

One of the main inhabitants of wetlands and riverbanks all over North America is the muskrat, a small furry rodent that is used commercially as a source of soft fur. Beaver, otter, raccoon, and wild mink also inhabit wetlands and are trapped for their fur. For other mammals, wetlands are primarily stopping places where they can be assured of food and water. In the West, coyotes tend to hang around wetlands, knowing that an abundance of prey will be available.

Thousands of plants and animals need the wetlands for part or all of their life cycles. Many types of fish spawn in wetlands, and then the young fish, called fry, swim out to sea, or perhaps into lakes, when they are big enough. Other types of fish spawn in the sea but the young move into coastal wetlands to take advantage of the rich food resources there. A major part of the world's fish catch is made up of species that use the wetlands at some time during their lives. Oysters and other shellfish that live in brackish water rely on the food sources in coastal wetlands.

Natural Water Managers

Wetlands are a vital habitat for wildlife, but they are also very important to people.

Muskrats (right) *live in wetland habitats all their lives. Several million muskrat pelts valued at $30 million or more are collected each year. Salmon* (left) *hatch out in estuaries and rivers but then go out into the ocean or lakes for most of their adult lives.*

Floodwater Storage. During the rainy season, streams and rivers become swollen with water. The extra water overflows into the natural wetlands beyond their banks. Floodwater is stored in these "bathtubs" until the water level in the waterways goes down. Slowly the water from the swamps, marshes, and floodplains is released back into the river or stream. This water-storage ability prevents flooding that might endanger fields and towns. Wetlands also lessen the erosion of the riverbanks by floodwaters.

In farm country, wetlands reduce the likelihood of crops being flooded. In urban areas they hold the water so that it doesn't pour into basements of homes. If you live in an area that frequently floods, chances are the wetlands around the area have been filled in. Only recently have towns begun to create artificial marshes to reduce flooding.

In the temperate zone, such flood control is vital. In the spring when the winter's accumulation of snow thaws, the waters head for lower land. Wetlands absorb this excess water like a sponge. They release it into the rivers during drier periods even if it means drying up themselves. Most wetland plants and animals have learned to adjust to these alternating wet and dry periods. Often their breeding periods are timed to the season they prefer.

Along seacoasts, especially those of Louisiana and Florida and such countries as Bangladesh, the coastal wetlands have an additional task—they absorb the initial blow when a hurricane strikes. The wetlands absorb the water driven ashore by the storm, as well as much of

Sedges are wetland plants that have unique leaves and roots that allow them to withstand changing water levels. This sedge meadow can store floodwater and then release it slowly.

the fury of the storm. The 150-mile (240-kilometer)-per-hour winds are lessened somewhat by crossing over the coastal marshes and swamps before they reach human developments. And wetlands don't suffer as much from the storm as structures often do.

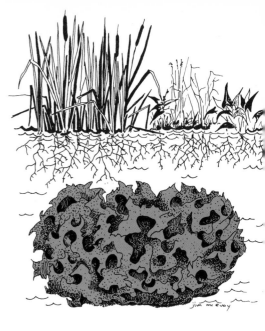

Recharging Groundwater. After a particularly dry year, you may have heard someone say, "The water table is very low." Groundwater is water held in soil and rock deep in the ground. The water table is the top of that layer of water. It is usually underground and invisible, but it reaches the surface in rivers and lakes. Towns built far from lakes or large rivers depend on groundwater for drinking water. People dig wells and may use electric pumps to bring this water to the surface.

The sediment in a wetland acts like a sponge to soak up and hold water.

When it rains, wetlands hold the water until it has a chance to seep back into the ground, recharging or refilling the groundwater supply. This may happen quickly or it could take many years.

Water Quality. People tend to settle near water. Industrial plants are built along rivers. Housing developments are often constructed as close to a coastline as possible. Towns and cities spring up near waterways.

In spring and fall, wetlands can replenish, or recharge, the groundwater.

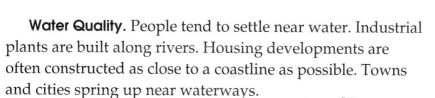

WETLAND

WATER TABLE

GROUNDWATER FLOW

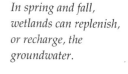

LAKE OR STREAM

Enormous quantities of waste are produced by so many people and their industries. People have often decided to just let the flow of a river carry it away. But where is "away"? "Away" usually means into wetlands or oceans. Wetlands have an amazing ability to store pollutants and prevent them from damaging the land (at least until the pollutant load is so heavy that it kills the wetland).

FACT

Two acres (0.8 hectare) of wetland can do as good a job of purifying water as a $150,000 sewage-disposal plant, perhaps even better because the sand and gravel used in the plant aren't very effective filters. The muddy bottom of a wetland can really trap pollutants and keep them from entering the groundwater.

Wetlands get a heavy dose of pollutants. If this happens gradually, the wetland community can usually handle it. Excess fertilizers (potash, nitrogen, and phosphorus) in the runoff from farms find their way to wetlands. There they are held, usually in the bottom mud. They may be absorbed by new living things and stored in the nutrient system.

But other chemicals do not make their way out of the wetlands. They stay. Chemicals known as PCBs, for example, were used by industry for many years before their toxic effects were discovered. PCBs tend to sink into the sediment of wetlands and just stay there. They will eventually have to be taken out and disposed of in some safer way.

Chesapeake Bay, one of the most important waterways on the East Coast, has suffered from deteriorating water quality for many years. One of the ways state and federal governments are helping to repair the water quality is by improving and protecting the wetlands in the entire watershed of the bay. The watershed covers parts of six states and includes 1.2 million acres (0.5 million hectare) of wetlands.

Pollution is trapped by the roots of the wetland plants.

Trapping Sediment. Millions of tons of topsoil are washed or blown into rivers each year and carried along with the flow. Most waterways in the Northern Hemisphere flow south. Eventually the water—and all that it carries—finds its way to the oceans or the Gulf of Mexico. Once the soil reaches those bodies of water, it may end up in the bottom of the ocean, lost to humans. Wetlands prevent that loss.

As a river meanders through the land, it occasionally overflows its banks as the riverbed curves. Wetlands form at those points in its course. And as the water moves through wetlands, it deposits the soil it is carrying. The fine soil particles settle to the bottom and give many marshes, swamps, and floodplains rich, fertile soil. If they didn't, people wouldn't be so quick to drain them for crop production.

Agricultural Value. Wetlands can be used for grazing cattle or for harvesting hay—any grass that can be cut and dried as feed and bedding for animals. Towns in early New England were often near wetlands that produced a cordgrass known as salt marsh hay. Actually, most marsh plants are

The water quality of Chesapeake Bay (above) is important for humans. But many rare and common species depend on it also. Studies have shown that some plants can help improve water quality by acting as pollution filters. Water hyacinths (right), for example, absorb nutrients such as nitrogen and phosphorus. However, they have a tendency to grow too fast and take over waterways, causing trouble.

suitable for hay. They also are high in protein and grow even when the surrounding area is experiencing a drought.

Research is being done on the uses of various wetland plants that grow in such abundance. The water hyacinth, for example, can be made into fertilizer, animal food, methane gas, and pulpboard. Cattails can yield large quantities of protein-rich flour from the flowers. In addition, the roots contain edible starch and even the young leaves are edible in salad. Older leaves are used as reeds for making baskets.

Calming Nature's Extremes. If you live on a lakeshore or seacoast, you know that the air temperature in these areas doesn't go to extremes. Water takes longer to heat up and to cool off than soil does. So a wetland area does a good job of moderating the temperature of a region.

Coastal wetlands take the punch out of violent storms. In spite of the beating they take from hurricanes and typhoons, wetlands seem to survive with little damage.

The country of Bangladesh has about 120 million people

in an area no larger than Wisconsin, so when disaster hits, it affects a huge number of people. In 1990 millions of people were made homeless by a typhoon only to have the monsoons flood out millions more. Disease followed in the storms' wake, and the country was devastated. For decades, the mangroves along the Bangladesh coastline were cut down. This destroyed the storm buffer zone. In areas where mangrove swamps still exist, there are rarely human deaths when a violent storm drives up the Bay of Bengal.

Food and Industrial Products

Besides providing a wealth of food for animals, wetlands produce edible products for humans. Rice, a staple food for millions of people, must grow in a watery habitat. However, rice lands are usually drained and then reflooded, to make the wetlands needed for growing more controllable.

Cranberries and blueberries thrive in bogs. Estuaries give us tons of shellfish, such as oysters, crab, clams, and shrimp. In the United States alone, commercial fisheries harvest more than $10 billion worth of fish every year. These include flounder, striped bass, salmon, bluefish, and killifish. Such fish use the estuaries, salt marshes, and coastal areas as spawning grounds.

Careful management of wetlands allows them to be used for aquaculture—the deliberate production of such foods as catfish. Crayfish, bullfrogs, as well as bait fish such as minnows, are also raised.

Wetlands are useful, productive places that are important to the functioning of our entire planet. But throughout history, people have not placed much value on them, preferring instead to eliminate them whenever possible.

The menhaden is a commercial estuarine fish that is used for fish meal and oil. It is also used in a wide range of nonfood products such as paint.

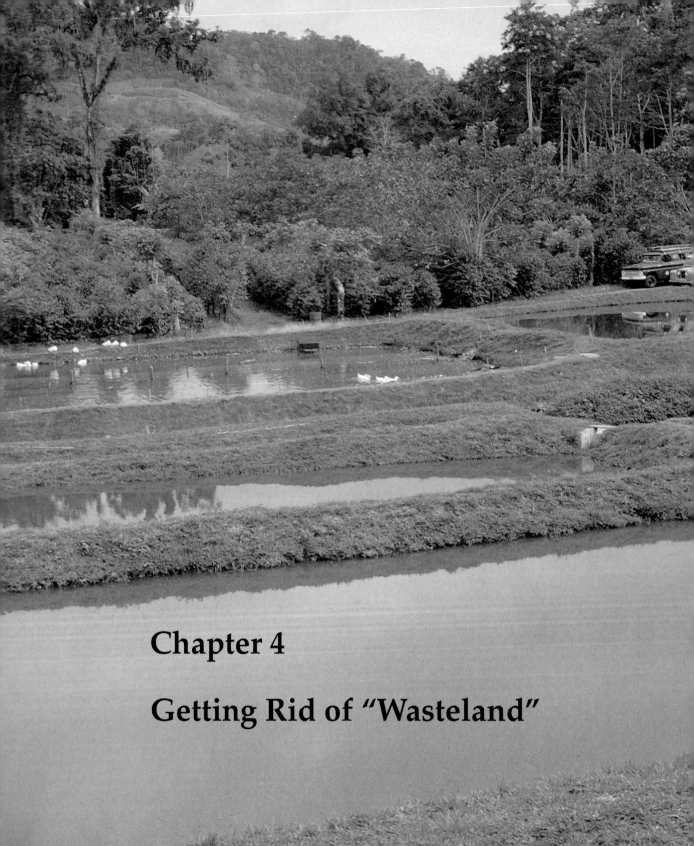

Chapter 4

Getting Rid of "Wasteland"

THE NETHERLANDS IS A LAND almost completely reclaimed from the sea and the rivers running into it. It is very flat and much of it is below sea level. Starting in the eleventh century, when its population began to expand, work began on reclaiming land. Much of the northern part was originally the delta of the Rhine River. It became the Zuiderzee, a huge inland sea that spread its waters into vast marshes. The southern part by Belgium was mostly peat bogs.

Holland, as part of the Netherlands was called, became famous for its many windmills, which were used to pump water out of the land and into drainage canals. Over the centuries, the sea has been held back and the land gradually drained and prepared for agriculture. An important task of the government in that country is to keep the sea back and let the people have their land.

A large area of south-central Italy is called the Pontine Marshes. Various popes and emperors of Italy tried throughout the centuries to drain the land, but it wasn't until about 1930 that the Fascist dictator Benito Mussolini managed to get the area drained. He brought in colonizing farm families, and today the area is one of the most productive vegetable-growing regions in Europe.

These are certainly very beneficial reasons for draining wetland. Land is of value to nations and individuals. Throughout history, people have thought that when they drained or filled wetlands, they were not "destroying" wetlands but were rescuing land for human benefit. But we know now that wetlands themselves are valuable and have benefit, both to the natural world and to human life.

In the United States, serious wetland reclamation began

Droughts occur naturally, and usually for a short period of time, but their consequences can be permanent. Wildlife usually suffers before humans.

in the middle 1800s, when Congress passed the Swamp Lands Act. This legislation gave 65 million acres (26 million hectares) of wetlands to the states. Wetlands could be reclaimed for agriculture, industry, or housing.

Forces of Destruction

Everything in nature is dynamic—it continually changes or evolves. For example, soil particles are picked up in one place, carried by the wind, and dropped somewhere else. Over time a lake becomes a pond and then a marsh. The flow of a river slows and allows extra salt water to filter into freshwater areas. All these are slow processes that may take thousands of years. Plants and animals have time to adapt.

Human beings, however, use rapid, unnatural ways to destroy or pollute wetlands. Plants and animals cannot adapt quickly enough to survive. They either become endangered—with only a few surviving—or they become extinct, disappearing forever.

The major needs of the human race—food, water, and shelter—have always been met in whatever ways people could find. In recent decades, the "needs" have expanded to include things that older civilizations never had the technology to do—keeping rivers from flooding, for example. Or

56

quicker travel on winding roads and rivers. Such "needs" have sometimes been met by making changes in the land, often at the cost of harm to wetlands.

At the mouth of the Mississippi River, a delta has been forming for thousands of years. It is part of the vast floodplain of the "Father of Waters," as the Mississippi has long been called. During normal spring flooding, the river has always spilled its excess water and silt onto the lands on either side. Over 4 million acres (1.6 million hectares) of the central United States were covered with rich, alluvial soil as a result of this flooding. Alluvial soil is formed by running water. This floodplain has developed through the centuries into huge bottomland forests.

In the last 70 years, almost all the trees that thrived in these bottomlands have been cut down. Humans put in levees (barriers) and dug canals to keep the land from flooding. Thousands of acres were drained and planted. This kind of conversion is a large example of what has been going on all over North America as communities grew, new farmland was needed, and people wanted more roads to travel through the countryside.

When channels or drainage ditches are dug into existing wetlands, the standing water can drain off, destroying the wetland.

A large amount of the farmland in Louisiana has been reclaimed from wetlands formed in the Mississippi delta.

Farming on Wetlands. Worldwide the growth of agriculture is the major cause of the disappearance of wetlands. In the United States, however, 87 percent of all freshwater wetland loss is related to agriculture.

Millions of acres of wet ground in the United States and southern Canada have been covered with corn and wheat. Cultivation has taken its toll on these prairie wetlands. Before 1990, over 40 percent of the prairie potholes in the central part of the continent were drained or filled.

It costs a farmer money any time his machinery has to stop moving in a straight line and go around a prairie pothole. It costs even more if a machine gets bogged down in a wet area. It costs a farmer some of his grain when waterfowl take up residence in a nearby wetland area and feed in his fields. And it costs him when he owns land that he can't use for growing things.

It's usually simple for the farmer to solve the problem. He just has to wait until autumn, when his crop is all in, or for a dry year and dig drainage ditches from the potholes to the nearest stream or river. By spring, the land is dry and he has increased the size of his productive fields.

FACT

Over 50 percent of the water consumed in America is used to raise grains and hay to feed livestock. It takes 1,000 times more water to produce a 10-pound (4.5-kilogram) beef roast than to grow 10 pounds of grain.

Investigating a Food Chain

How many acres of corn and hay are needed to raise a calf up to a 900-pound (408-kilogram) steer, at which time it would probably be butchered? Ask a farmer how many bushels of corn and hay he uses weekly to feed his cattle or to use for bedding? How many beef cows does he feed with this amount? How many acres did the farmer cultivate to raise this amount?

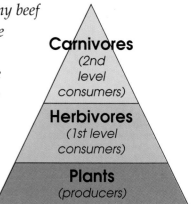

When a steer is butchered, how many pounds of meat are produced? Consult a meat-packing plant for the figures. The fur, bones, hooves, and most internal organs are not edible.

Now study a calorie chart. How many calories are there in a 5-pound (2.2-kilogram) roast, a hamburger, and a pork or lamb chop? How many calories do you need to live and grow each day? Each month? Each year?

Put all these data together. Suppose that you ate nothing but meat to stay alive for one year (which would not be healthy). How many cows would you need? How many acres of grain would it take to feed these cows?

By now you should be asking what you can do about this tremendous loss of energy in the food chain. One simple solution is to eat more vegetables, fruits, and grains, reducing your meat consumption.

Now calculate the calories in a cup of corn, beans, cereal, and a variety of fruits. Calculate how many calories of these foods you would need to stay alive for one year. How many acres of land are needed to produce this amount? One apple tree or one nut tree takes little room on an acre.

The cattle that many people in the wealthier countries eat as a main part of their diet are fed grains and other plants that could be used to feed humans. People are at the top of the food chain.

Humans in the Food Chain. We need to look at where humans fit into the food chain. Plants are the only living things that can make their own food. They are the producers. Cattle eat plants. They are called first-level consumers. Humans, who are second-level consumers, eat beef from cattle. Americans eat more meat than people in any other country in the world. Hamburgers, chops, and roasts are regarded as necessary to our diet. This puts us high on the food chain.

In Bangladesh, over 80 million acres (32 million hectares) of wetland areas are now covered with crops for that country's growing population. On the delta near the Bay of Bengal, about 55,000 square miles (142,000 square kilometers) have been "reclaimed" for rice, which grows well in wet, soggy ground.

Coastal mangrove swamps have been destroyed in Asia and replaced with rice paddies to feed growing populations.

In the prairie lands of North America, fields are often plowed in the fall. The topsoil lies exposed all winter to blustery winds, rains, and, in spring, to melting snows. The wind and the water pick up tiny particles of soil, rock, and mineral, and carry them along as sediment. Finally the sediment is dumped into streams and rivers. The rivers overflow into marshes, swamps, and other wetlands. As the running water slows, the sediment is deposited.

Sediment carries the valuable nutrients that form rich topsoil in floodplains and deltas. In many wetlands, however, the sediment can cause damage. The fine particles get into the gills of fish and clog the shells of mollusks. Oysters and clams close up and stop feeding. Thousands of aquatic animals are killed by muddy waters. In addition, sediment speeds up the filling in of the wetlands. Plowed fields near a wetland can gradually cause it to disappear.

Mollusks, such as mussels, open their shells to filter large quantities of water for oxygen and food. If the water is polluted, they close their shells and stop feeding.

Waterworks

There is a great demand on the world's freshwater supply. Less than 3 percent of all the water on Earth is fresh—and potentially drinkable—and more than 20 percent of that water is underground. That leaves very little fresh water in lakes, rivers, wetlands, and other waterways above the ground.

The world has a limited supply of fresh water to go around. Life in the wetlands is the first to suffer when water

California's wetlands have almost disappeared while irrigation water flows through miles of aqueducts to central valley farmland.

becomes scarce. The world's population is now at 5.3 billion. It is estimated that this number will climb to over 6 billion by the year 2000. Where are all those people going to get fresh water to drink?

Humans do not generally use the water from wetlands directly. Instead, they dam, dike, and channel the fresh waters from rivers which cannot then supply enough water to nearby wetlands. The wetlands begin to dry up.

Over 80 percent of the water used in California alone goes to water crops that are distributed throughout the nation. The use of water to irrigate agricultural lands has dried up more than 85 percent of the wetlands in that state.

The West's Special Problem. Biologists in the West first discovered that they had a major problem when they began discovering waterfowl with many serious mutations— changes in the genes that produced defective young. They found blind birds, wingless ducks, deformed fish. This all came to light at Kesterson National Wildlife Refuge in California's San Joaquin Valley.

In a hunt for causes, they finally found that levels of selenium, a natural—and essential—chemical element in the soils, had increased until it had become a poison.

Millions of years ago volcanoes spewed selenium out into the mud of inland seas. The mud eventually hardened and became shale rock. Over time, this shale, through folding and faulting of the Earth's crust, arrived at the surface.

But the trouble did not begin until California's increasing

population sought more farmland. Federally supported projects were begun to "make the desert bloom." Engineers harnessed water sources and irrigated the dry, exposed desert, making new farmland. But water running off the farmland flowed over selenium-bearing rocks. The poisonous selenium, along with arsenic, another toxic element, was picked up by the water and carried into the wetlands at lower elevations. The damage began.

This salty California desert used to be a productive wetland in the Kesterson Wildlife Refuge. Selenium and arsenic in the rocks was exposed by water projects that were meant to make the land productive.

Similar selenium-bearing rock is located in patches throughout western North America. And much of it is located in areas where major irrigation projects have been built. It's possible that in the future formerly productive land may have to be retired so that irrigation doesn't leach selenium from the soil and send it to poison wetlands. Or farmers may develop irrigation methods that do not concentrate such chemicals.

The U.S. Army Corps of Engineers

The United States Army Corps of Engineers is a section of the army that is responsible for projects involving America's waterways. The corps built levees, locks, and dams. It dredged rivers and harbors to improve shipping. It built dams for hydroelectric power. It developed city water supply facilities. And it even fixed up rivers and lakes as recreation areas.

The Army Corps of Engineers originated in 1775 during the American Revolution, when it built forts and mapped lands for battles. In 1819 the corps was given the job of improving America's land and water transportation.

In 1824, the corps began to dredge the Ohio and Mississippi rivers and straighten bends to simplify boat travel. When they began construction projects to prevent floods, they got a reputation as the "concrete-pouring river-channeling beast" or the "people that plug everything up."

In 1927 there was a disastrous flood of the lower Mississippi, when 25,000 square miles (65,000 square kilometers) were flooded, more than 2,000 people were killed, and half a million were left homeless. Congress authorized the corps to carry out massive water-control measures including levees, dredging, and floodways. When the Mississippi floods, the control structures divert flood water down the Atchafalaya River. But during normal water flow, most of the Mississippi's waters are forced toward New Orleans because the Atchafalaya River was naturally getting more and more of the Mississippi's flow. If that had happened, the lower Mississippi would have become an estuary and the economies of the river cities would have been destroyed.

This experience started the Army Corps of Engineers working on flood control all over the country. All of this has been very beneficial to a lot of people—but often not

Before the Old River control structure was built, the Mississippi River was changing its course and flowing through Old River and down the Atchafalaya River, which flows many miles west of New Orleans. The Mississippi's flow is now forced to go past New Orleans and down into the Gulf of Mexico.

Oil and gas companies dredge canals through Louisiana's wetlands for exploration. Too many dredged canals can destroy valuable marshes by gradually turning them into open water.

so beneficial to the wetlands that were affected. In 1986, the United States Environmental Protection Agency acquired responsibility for the protection of wetland areas.

But it's too late for some places.

Channelization, Dredging, and Levees. Channelization is the straightening of streams and rivers. It is often done to control the flooding of a moving body of water. However, channeling may also be done to improve navigation. Indian canoes have been replaced by huge barges. A wider, deeper, and shorter river gives ships a shorter distance to travel from one destination to another.

Machines called dredgers dig up the bottoms and shorelines of the waterways to make them deeper, wider, and straighter. The mud taken from the bottom is moved to the curves and bends to fill them in.

During channelization, trees and shrubs along the banks are removed. Then these banks are built up into levees or dikes, which are barriers that prevent the passage of water. Usually the banks are covered with cement to stop erosion.

One of the effects of this work is to make the water flow faster. There are no muddy banks and tree roots to slow it down. But removing trees from shorelines also cuts down on the nutrients being carried because no leaves fall into the water. And with no shade, water temperature increases. All these factors affect the wetlands and nearby habitats.

When a stream has been straightened between levees, flooding on either side of it is reduced. The wetlands dry up. The animals must migrate to find another wetland, become dormant in the dry mud, or die. For plant and animal life that cannot adapt quickly, channelization means death.

An Earth Experience

Just Waiting for a Drink

Is all lost when a marsh, swamp, or shallow pond dries up? Not necessarily. Many aquatic plants go through a season or two of being dormant.

During a dry spell in summer, locate a pond or other wet area that has dried up. Scoop a few inches of soil from the bottom and place it in a glass bowl or jar. Cover the soil with distilled water. Don't use tap water because it may have chemicals in it that would affect the plants. Place your sample in a warm, sunny spot.

Different forms of algae will gradually come back to life in the water. Locate an algae identification book from your school's learning center to help you identify the specimens in your watery community. Cladophora will probably appear first. Oscillatoria takes about a month and Volvox even longer. These are all microscopic algae. Larger algae, such as Chara and Nitella, may also have survived the drought conditions. You will need to use a microscope to study some of the smallest types, and you will also discover many small invertebrate animals that hatch their eggs in the soils.

The Kissimmee River Story

Florida's Kissimmee River shows how channeling can cause major damage to the environment. The Indians named the twisting river Kissimmee, meaning "long water," because it wound through over 103 miles (166 kilometers) of wetlands to Lake Okeechobee, which is only 50 miles (80 kilometers) south. Lake Kissimmee is the northernmost part of the watershed that includes the Everglades. It's also an important source of fresh water for Florida's aquifer.

But the Kissimmee tended to flood very easily, and when hurricanes passed through the area, a great deal of damage was done. As the population boomed in the 1960s, people wanted flood control and more recreational areas. So the state of Florida and U.S. Corps of Engineers began a ten-year project to straighten the river. Eventually it was only 56 miles (90 kilometers) long, 300 feet (92 meters) wide, and 30 feet (9.2 meters) deep. It took millions of dollars and almost ten years to get the kinks out of the river.

But before the work was even finished, it was clear that the channeling had damaged the whole of southern Florida.

The meandering Kissimmee River in Florida was shortened and changed into a straight canal by channelization. But the new, straighter river did so much damage to the environment that the process is now being reversed.

Straightening the Kissimmee River destroyed over 40,000 acres (16,000 hectares) of beautiful marshes. People living near the "new" Kissimmee built canals so that they could have their own waterfront. This destroyed many thousands of additional acres of wetlands and their abundant wildlife.

Permanent and wintering waterfowl disappeared, finding the new river lacking in food and quiet rest areas. There were fewer fish in the river. In addition, the water quality of Lake Okeechobee, which feeds the Everglades, was degraded. The straightening had created more land for cattle ranching. Runoff from that land increased the nutrient levels, especially of the element phosphorus, in the water that flowed into Lake Okeechobee.

Experiments were begun in 1984 to test methods for returning the Kissimmee to its previous twisting, marshy state. The engineers kept the deep center channel in certain places and then let the river run back into its old, shallow riverbed. And instead of managing the water level, they let it return to varying with the seasons.

As part of the Kissimmee River restoration project, three steel dams, called weirs, were built to divert water from the canal back into the original river channel and floodplain. The gap in the center allows small boats to still use the main channel.

The work has a long way to go because the state still has to finish purchasing the land that was turned into cattle ranches. Also, the Corps of Engineers' work has not been completely funded. Eventually they hope to have 32,000 acres (13,000 hectares) of marshland turned back into wetland habitat.

Channelization and other drainage techniques have reduced the 130 million acres (52 million hectares) of wetlands in United States to less than 75 million acres (30 million hectares). The U.S. Soil Conservation Service plans to channelize 8,000 more watersheds before the year 2000, further reducing America's wetlands.

FACT

The Louisiana Situation. Over two-thirds of the entire nation's annual losses of coastal wetlands occur in Louisiana, an average of 32,000 acres (13,000 hectares). That state's coastal swamps and marshes are vital to the survival of a number of animal species. For example, about one-fourth of North America's puddle ducks winter there. About 30 percent of the U.S. commercial fish catch comes from their waters. In addition, Louisiana has the nation's largest fur and alligator harvest, though these are becoming increasingly less important as people object to the killing of such animals.

Levees along the Mississippi are blocking the addition of the new sediment and fresh water that is needed to maintain healthy coastal marshes. Fresh water is needed to maintain the right amount of

The Caernarvon diversion structure in Louisiana sends fresh water from the Mississippi River into nearby saltmarshes to maintain proper salinity.

salinity to keep plants healthy. Additional sediment is needed to build up the marsh floor. But the sediment is being trapped upstream in reservoirs or rushed out to sea in channelized rivers.

Many scientists think that the Earth is getting warmer. If that is so, the level of the sea will rise because water expands as it warms. That expansion will put the coastal marshes of Louisiana in still greater danger of being destroyed by salt water.

Dams and Reservoirs. Electric power can be produced by using flowing water to turn giant turbines. When a dam is built across a river, the water backs up in a lake-like area called a reservoir. When electricity is to be made, the water is released from the reservoir down a tunnel inside the dam. The motion given the water by gravity is used to turn the turbines. The water, its energy spent, is then released into the lower part of the river.

The Imperial Dam on the Colorado River provides irrigation water for Arizona and California, but it has helped stop natural sediment flow and destroyed riverine wetlands.

Unfortunately, the construction of a dam and its reservoir usually involves the destruction of wetlands and the animals and plants that live in them. But the damage doesn't stop there.

As Cities and Industry Develop

Over one-half of the world's people live within 125 miles (201 kilometers) of a coast. Can the huge human population on the edges of continents live in harmony with the natural environment?

The growth of a city near water involves many things—draining and filling for harbor facilities, building factories, finding enough space (and the right space) for landfills for waste, constructing warehouses, airports, and housing, building roads and shopping centers.

In the process of all this construction, wetlands are often changed to drylands. In Canada, wetland destruction due to urban development has occurred along the shores of the St. Lawrence River, the lower Great Lakes, and the east and west coasts. More than 90 percent of the marshes along Lake Ontario have been rapidly depleted because of urban and industrial development along the shores, especially along the heavily populated western shore from the Niagara River to Oshawa.

In western Canada, logging puts heavy stresses on estuaries, where logs are often cut, handled, and stored. Of concern is the estuary of the Fraser River. It has the largest salmon runs in the world, supports the largest population of wintering waterfowl in Canada, and is the main stopping point for birds on the Pacific Flyway. Vancouver, which faces the Fraser Delta, is growing dramatically.

Living Along Water. People enjoy living in sight of water, and they are always in conflict with other inhabitants of the coastal or river wetlands. Most coastal wetlands lost in Florida between 1950 and 1970 went for urban development. In 1950 hundreds of thousands of acres of mangrove swamps along the southern coastline were cut. The swamps were filled in to make way for condominiums, houses, and marinas for boating.

The suburbs around Chicago were built on a floodplain created when Lake Chicago, now called Lake Michigan, was 60 feet (18.3 meters) higher than it is today. Over thousands of years, this enormous lake regularly spilled into the surrounding land. The rich, productive soil left behind is now covered with buildings and highways.

The counties in the Chicago area need all the wetlands available to handle the constant threat of flooding from the streams and rivers that extend out from the lake. The Des Plaines and the DuPage Rivers, for example, flood regularly. In fact, the Des Plaines River is having some of its zigs and

Before World War II, Gulf Shores, Alabama (left), consisted of one row of tiny cottages. After bridges and highways were built, huge hotels and condominiums replaced the cottages, sand dunes, and coastal wetlands. This interstate highway cloverleaf in Louisiana (below) was constructed over an area that was once wetlands.

zags restored to cut down on the flooding.

The once-vast coastal wetlands around San Francisco Bay have shrunk as industrial and residential development has increased. However, these coastal wetlands still support thirteen federally listed endangered species including the peregrine falcon, bald eagle, brown pelican, and clapper rail. The area also provides spawning, nursery space, and food for more than fifty species of marine fish that are themselves food for fish-eating birds like cormorants.

Highway Construction. In the prairie pothole regions, highway construction has destroyed numerous wetlands. When highways are constructed directly through wetlands, outlet or drainage ditches drain the water. If a highway is constructed close to farms and near highway drainage ditches, farmers use the drainage ditches meant for the highway to drain wetlands on their properties. One study noted that when a road or highway is built near wetlands, 64 acres (26 hectares) of wetlands are lost for every 100 miles (161 kilometers) of highway. Most of this loss comes from farmers taking advantage of highway drainage ditches.

Removing the Forests

Forests serve as watersheds. Their complex systems of spreading roots hold water in the soil during the wet seasons and release it during dry spells. This provides a relatively steady supply of moisture to the surrounding land, often including wetland areas.

Deforestation—the removal of trees from an area—leaves the soil exposed and open to erosion by wind and water. Tons of particles of soil are washed into streams, rivers,

White cedar is logged in Northern Michigan swamps during the winter and is usually not replanted.

reservoirs, swamps, and estuaries, where they settle to the bottom as sediment. Many man-made reservoirs are filling in fast. Some in Southeast Asia and Latin America are almost useless because of big-scale removal of trees surrounding them. The reservoirs that supply water to the locks in the Panama Canal may be filled in by the year 2000.

In Canada, large amounts of black spruce are harvested each year in wetland areas. In fact, in southern Ontario, almost 20 million acres (7.9 million hectares) of forest are made up of peat-dominated wetlands.

Mangroves. Millions of acres of mangrove trees have been harvested worldwide for wood, fuel, urbanization, agricultural land, and to construct fish and shellfish ponds for a process called *aquaculture*. The Philippines had almost 2,000 square miles (5,100 square kilometers) of mangroves in 1920. In 1988, the count was down to 150 square miles (380 square kilometers). Most of these swamps were clear-cut for timber, tannin, or aquaculture ponds.

In Indonesia, the mangroves were cut down for timber and wood chips and for water ponds to cultivate prawns, shrimp, and fish. Many mangroves have been cut in order to raise rice, but this crop does not grow well in the salty mud.

Java's north coast was once lined with mangrove swamps. It, too, has been deforested and converted for aquaculture. Specially built ponds called tambaks raise shrimp and other shellfish. Such conversion has caused the coast to degrade and erode. With the mangroves gone, the commercial fish catch is reduced, so fishing communities build more tambaks, thus destroying more mangroves. This vicious cycle continues until, within a few years, the ponds lose their productivity. Then the Javanese people repeat the whole process somewhere else.

Australians, on the other hand, are taking care of their mangrove swamps. The native aborigines do the harvesting because they know how to live with the swamps without destroying them. The swamps continue to provide the nursery for commercial fishing. They also serve as a barrier to keep the ocean from eroding the coastline.

Humans destroy wetlands in many ways and for many reasons. But the wildlife doesn't care about the reason. They only experience the loss of their homes and food supplies—and their new generations.

Schools of young fish hide in red mangrove prop roots. Mangroves not only provide irreplaceable habitat for fish and invertebrates, but also protect coastal shorelines from erosion and storms and produce food for animals in the estuarine food chain.

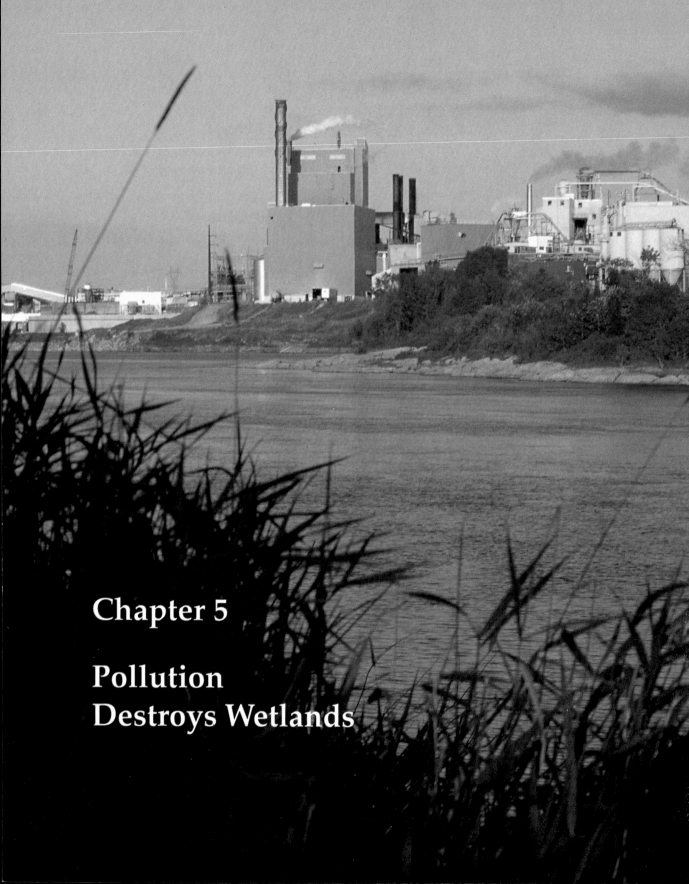

Chapter 5

Pollution
Destroys Wetlands

HUMANS HAVE REDUCED the number or quantity of wetlands by many methods. These wetlands and their habitats are gone. But we also destroy the quality of the wetlands that remain. This is called wetland degradation. The wetlands may survive, but pollutants poison them. They become as useless to living things as if they did not exist at all.

Although it is illegal in the United States to deliberately pollute wetlands, harmful substances get into them by people dumping things into rivers and lakes—called point pollution—and by runoff—nonpoint pollution. Nonpoint pollution consists of chemicals that enter a wetland through rainwater that runs off land, carrying fertilizers, pesticides, or oil from roads with it.

The livestock raised in the United States alone produces around 2 billion tons (1.8 billion metric tons) of wastes every year. Most of it is liquid or is dissolved by rain and runs off into both surface and groundwater.

FACT

Overdosed on Fertilizer. The use of fertilizer on farms, gardens, and lawns increased tremendously in the last half of the 1900s. In 1950 there were 14 million tons (12.6 million metric tons) applied to the land in the United States. In 1990 the figure reached 140 million tons (126 million metric tons).

Fertilizers do not stay put. Almost half of them run off into surrounding waters, evaporate, or get washed out of the soil. They contain heavy doses of nitrogen and phosphates, which cause a rapid increase in algae and other aquatic plants.

An Earth Experience

Investigating Marsh Plants

In late spring, take a hike to a nearby marsh, drainage ditch, or pond. Carry along a large, wide-mouthed glass jar to hold the specimens you collect.

Collect a variety of aquatic plants such as duckweed, strands of algae, lily pads, chara, milfoil, and other unique species. Also dig up a couple of the plants rooted in the mud. Carry them back to your "laboratory" in the jar filled with the same water.

Pour off the floating plants into a temporary container. Anchor the rooted plants on the bottom of the jar with a few pebbles and sand. Return the floating plants and water to your jar. They should form a thick, dense mat across the surface of the water.

Cut out all light to your "pond" except through the top by taping black construction paper around the jar. Set the open jar in a sunny window for two weeks. Then remove the paper and study all the plants. Are the rooted plants still healthy and green? Look at the bottom of the floating plants. What happened to the layers that were below the surface? When surface plants black out the sun, the bottom plants have a tough time.

It is hard to imagine that fertilizer, which is food for growing plants, can also be a pollutant. There are solutions to the problem, however. Farmers can rotate crops and reduce the amount of commercial fertilizer they use. Homeowners can use grass clippings as natural fertilizer.

Pesticide Damage. Poisonous chemicals are used to kill insects, fungi, weeds, and other pests. Most of these poisons,

called biocides, contaminate the soil, clouds, groundwater, and surface water, all of which meet in wetlands, which get more than their share of pesticides.

Many pesticides evaporate with water up into clouds, only to return to the ground when it rains. A federal study was conducted in 1991 on rainwater in 23 states. The study showed that in Illinois, for example, rainwater may contain almost twice as much poisonous pesticide as is allowed by EPA safety standards.

Pesticides raining down from the sky fall far away from the farm country where they were used. They showed up at test sites in the heart of a city and in the Isle Royale National Park in northern Lake Superior. The refreshing rain falling on wetlands helps restore the water level, but it may carry poison with it.

Currently the United States uses about 400,000 tons (360,000 metric tons) of pesticides every year. Less than 1 percent of these toxic chemicals actually affect the pests for which they were intended. The remainder goes into the environment.

FACT

Sewage from barnyards runs off into nearby waterways and on to adjacent wetlands, contaminating them for humans and wildlife.

Raw Sewage. For centuries individuals and towns located near rivers and oceans have dumped human waste into the waterways. They believed that the water would take care of dispersing the waste. And such disposal methods were certainly much cheaper than building a modern disposal plant.

But the towns have turned into cities, and overpopulated areas are finding out that the water bodies and their inhabitants cannot handle the amount of sewage being dumped into them.

In the United States, over 190 million tons (170 million metric tons) of human sewage are dumped off the Pacific, Atlantic, and Gulf coasts. This dumping has been legal. But much of the sewage comes back in to shore. The tides carry it into estuaries and bays. Shellfish from the Chesapeake Bay and Puget Sound in Washington are so contaminated with bacteria from sewage that they are unsafe to eat. As of 1993 it will be illegal for sewage to be dumped into the oceans.

In the Third World, at least 20 million people die every year of diseases carried by contaminated water. Many millions more suffer severely from waterborne disorders, such as diarrhea, blindness, or parasitic worms.

Hazardous Chemicals. Wastes from industry may pose some health or environmental hazards if they are discarded with regular garbage. These wastes come from chemical factories, iron and steel industries, metal foundries, paper mills, and oil refineries. The wastes include cyanide, mercury, arsenic, copper, lead, zinc, benzene, dioxin, and cadmium. The list could go on and on—and all of them can damage wetlands and their wildlife.

For many years, dangerous wastes were sealed in barrels, which were buried in landfills or dropped in the ocean. But no one has ever invented a barrel that won't eventually leak. In fact, many of them are leaking now. The poisonous liquids are running out into the soil and down into the drinking-water supplies. Sometimes companies just poured hazardous wastes directly into rivers or nearby wetland areas. That used to seem a reasonable thing to do because wetlands, after all, were just "wastelands."

General Electric Company in Pittsfield, Massachusetts, drained its waste material into a nearby river for many years until it was stopped in 1977. Very dangerous, cancer-causing chemicals called PCBs ended up in the sediment at the bottom of the river. Whenever the river flooded, this sediment was carried onto the floodplains and into a large pond along the river.

Today, we are aware that poisons have accumulated in some areas making them pits of poisons that endanger all life around them. Many of these areas are designated "Superfund" sites, which means that the federal government is paying to clean them up. Poisoned sediment in ponds and other wetlands can be dredged up, though not without considerable damage to the surroundings.

There are more than 70,000 disposal sites for hazardous wastes in the United States. Billions of

This abandoned hazardous-waste site in a wetland area contained buried drums that were brought to the surface by heavy rains.

gallons of liquid waste are dumped in these areas every day of the year, threatening the groundwater beneath the landfills, which are rarely really leakproof. The EPA has targeted over 900 landfills for attention.

The National Wildlife Federation reported that 500,000 tons (450,000 metric tons) of salt were used on the highways of the New England states in one year alone. New England has numerous wetland areas, some of them commercially important, such as the bogs where cranberries are grown.

Salt that Destroys

Wetlands along the coastal shores are naturally going to receive salt from the sea. Plants and animals that live in these communities have adapted to this half-salt, half-fresh environment. But the salinity of these wetlands is natural and not caused by humans.

The use of salt on roads to melt ice and snow is a different matter. In the northern United States and Canada, salt is often used in winter to raise the temperature of ice on slippery roads, making it thaw and thus less dangerous. However, that salt runs off the highways and goes into wetlands.

The trees in this marsh—once a thriving freshwater wetland—are dying from too much salt water flowing in. This is caused by rising sea levels.

Discovering How Salt Harms

Collect a stalk of Elodea, a common aquatic plant found in marshes and swamps. Its leaves are only two cells thick, easily seen under a microscope. Remove a small leaf near the top of the plant. Place it on a slide in a drop of water. Put a cover slip over it because you will be using high power on the microscope to identify the parts of an individual cell.

Notice the streaming chloroplastids, the green bodies that make food for the plant. You can see that the cytoplasm (the liquid part of the cell) is evenly distributed within the cell wall.

Now pollute the cells. Lift up the cover slip and sprinkle a few grains of salt on the leaf. Replace the cover slip and look through the microscope at what is happening. What does salt do to living cells? The loss of water from cells is called dehydration.

In the northern United States and Canada, salt that harms wetlands can also come from water itself. All water contains dissolved mineral salts. There are limits to the levels of salts allowed in drinking water—500 parts per million (ppm). Water used in irrigation can have up to 700 ppm. These salts are in the runoff from fields and accumulate in wetlands.

When nature is left alone, snow melting in spring at higher elevations sends water rushing into the river. It carries the salts away. But in many areas, dams hold back a lot of water. The salts accumulate along the waterway, making the water saltier and saltier as time goes on. And as the river flows, it dumps its salty water into wetlands. Salt makes the plants work less efficiently than they should.

83

Thermal Pollution

Many aquatic plants and animals cannot adjust to quick or extreme temperature changes. Heated water dumped into wetlands is called thermal pollution. The tiniest living organisms—the base of the food chain that supports all life in the wetland—are the first to be killed by a sudden increase in water temperature.

Water is used to cool machinery or products during various manufacturing processes. After the water has done its job, its temperature may be 15 to 25 degrees F. (8 to 14 degrees C) higher when it is released downstream. The Environmental Protection Agency has set limits on how warm water can be when it is released.

An Earth Experience

Getting in Hot Water

Hydras are tiny, stinging animals found attached to surfaces in fresh water. They are related to free-swimming jellyfish, which live in salt water. These animals are quite sensitive to the changes in water temperature.

Hydras are found in water that is relatively quiet. They do not survive well in swift-flowing streams or rivers. A marsh, swamp, or creek would be a good site for hydra hunting. Collect several plants and twigs from under water near the bank. Place these in a glass aquarium or large bowl. The base of a hydra is often attached to the stem of the plant. Because light can shine through them, they may be difficult to see. Hydras look like tiny tubes with branching tentacles on one end, around the mouth.

Use the water the hydra was living in to fill a small aquarium. Once the water has become still, the tiny animals will stretch out

Warm water carries less oxygen than cooler water. This reduces the numbers and kinds of animals that can survive in a heat-polluted area. The animals' respiration rate goes up as the temperature rises. This creates an even greater need for oxygen, just when there isn't as much oxygen available. Fish, snails, clams, and other animals literally suffocate in water that is warmer than they need. Many estuary animals have been killed by heat pollution from industry.

Oil Spills

Petroleum, or oil, is not found everywhere on the planet. So, ever since it was found to be useful, it has been transported in ships across oceans. More recently, engineers have

their jelly-like bodies to as much as 1/2 inch (about 1.2 centimeters) long. Count how many animals you managed to collect.

Place one twig with a hydra attached into a quart jar half filled with water. Take the temperature of the water. Now add warm water until you raise the temperature by 5 degrees Fahrenheit (2.8 degrees Celcius). Did the hydra lose its hold on the stick? Keep increasing the temperature until it does. This will give you some idea of the thermal tolerance of these animals and others like them.

drilled for oil in the coastal waters off continents. Oil and the products made from it are always being moved—from offshore wells to tankers, from land wells to pipelines, from refineries to distributors. Whenever oil is moved, there is a chance that some of it will spill. And much of a spill ends up in wetlands. On land it becomes part of the runoff into marshes. On the ocean it floats ashore and accumulates in coastal swamps and marshes.

Oil that enters a wetland does its damage in several ways. First, it coats the plants and whatever animals fail to get out of its way. The plants are then unable to absorb carbon dioxide or use sunlight to carry on photosynthesis, and they soon die. The animals suffocate very quickly. Those animals that come later, especially the birds that nest there, suffer in different ways. When they eat oil-coated seeds, the oil harms their digestive systems. Their eggs fail to develop if they get even a small amount of oil on the shells because the poisons go through the shell.

The controversy about the safety of offshore drilling has been going on for decades. Even the huge *Exxon Valdez* oil spill in Alaska in 1989 didn't stop the United States government from continuing to sell offshore rights to oil companies. Some areas go for $100 for every 5 acres (2 hectares). Drilling is going on right now in Bristol Bay in Alaska and Monterey Bay in California. Drilling on land is just as unlucky for wetlands. The Arctic National Wildlife Refuge of Alaska, with its fragile tundra, may be opened to drilling soon.

Not only are wetlands hurt when canals are dredged by oil companies, but, once oil rigs produce, spills also occur, further harming fragile wetland ecosystems.

The Wetland Invader

A plant with the odd name of purple loosestrife arrived in America from Europe in the 1800s. It came over aboard ships as seed accidentally mixed with sand. Before the ships left for Europe, they dumped the sand on coastal areas, and the seeds were free to grow.

Gradually, purple loosestrife invaded the northeastern United States, eastern Canada, and British Columbia. In other parts of Canada and the American Midwest, the tall, purple-flowering plant spread when people unknowingly planted it adjacent to waterways.

The problem is that purple loosestrife knocks native plants out of their habitats. Called the "beautiful killer" by the Canadian Wildlife Federation, purple loosestrife has no natural enemy in North America. The plant is tough and aggressive and very productive—one plant can produce many thousands of seeds in a growing season. It can quickly take over a wetland area, killing the natural vegetation.

In Canada particularly, efforts to control the marauding plant have been underway for some time. Scientists have tried burning, mowing, and even flooding. Herbicides work, but have serious side effects. Research goes on, but so far the only answer is to pull up the plant and burn it whenever you see one. If it's in a neighbor's yard, tell them about the problem this plant can cause and encourage them to get rid of this beautiful killer. At least one town has officially outlawed purple loosestrife, which is polluting the wetlands.

Pollution comes in many forms—chemical, fertilizer, and heat—and even foreign visitors who refuse to go home. Combined with the filling and draining that farmers and construction do, wetlands have a hard time surviving. But, as we'll see, they are worth fighting for.

Chapter 6

The Florida
Everglades Story

THE FLORIDA EVERGLADES is a huge enchanted wonderland like nowhere else on Earth. A human intruder in the midst of the marsh would see the green of the sawgrass that fills the water blend at the horizon with the blue of the Florida sky. Many of the swamp's plants and animals are unknown elsewhere. And some of them are in danger of dying out.

The Everglades of a hundred years ago was one of the natural wonders of the world. The swamp stretched 100 miles (161 kilometers) from Lake Okeechobee in the north to the Gulf of Mexico and the Bay of Florida in the south. It spread 30 to 75 miles (48 to 120.6 kilometers) wide, covering 4,000 square miles (10,360 square kilometers). What has happened to the Everglades and what the plans are for its future is the story of wetlands everywhere.

The Everglades is not just one kind of wetland. It includes wet prairie, marshes, rivers, freshwater swamps, coastal mangrove swamps, and even pine woods. Basically, however, it is a big, grass-filled sheet of water, usually less than 2 feet (61 centimeters) deep. The water moves slowly southward like a wide river of grass. In fact, the Seminole Indian name for the Glades meant "grassy waters." The land is very flat, dropping only 20 feet (6 meters) from Lake Okeechobee to the gulf.

Today, things are changing, due primarily to the damage humans have done. The Everglades has now shrunk by 1,300 square miles (3,367 square kilometers), almost one-third of its original size. The southern part of the area has been set aside

The Everglades takes up most of south Florida. Population pressures in the area affect the Everglades, and the presence of the Everglades affects all of south Florida.

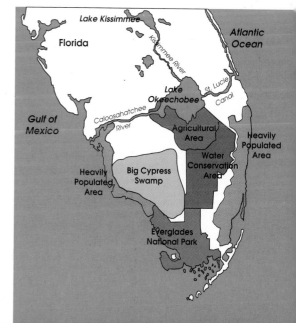

During much of the year, there are areas of open water (left) *peeking through the clumps of sawgrass and trees. But at other times, the prairie* (right) *is so dry that the tree islands called hammocks can catch fire.*

as Everglades National Park. But even the park cannot be preserved completely. It is affected by the growth of Miami on the east and agriculture and housing on the north.

The Plants of the Everglades. There are over 1,000 different plant species in the Everglades. Much of it is flat prairie, consisting primarily of tall sawgrass, a sedge plant, as far as the eye can see. Sawgrass is thick, stiff, and sharp enough to cut through flesh or cloth. Walking through sawgrass can be a painful experience.

The flat sawgrass scene is dotted with occasional tree islands, called hammocks. On these higher and dryer elevations, fairly common trees are found: the royal palm, oaks, pines, mahogany, and strangler fig. Other trees don't mind having their feet in the water. Bald cypress, tupelo, and live oak make up the freshwater swamp areas. As the swamp moves into the brackish areas near the Gulf Coast, different trees take over, especially mangroves. To the north of Everglades National Park is Big Cypress Preserve, a swamp in which Seminole Indians still live.

The famed Spanish moss that hangs from the trees adds a look of mystery to the landscape. Long thought to be a parasite that feeds off other plants, we now know that this

tangled, gray, long-stemmed relative of the pineapple is an epiphyte—a plant with roots that take moisture from the air. Other related plants called bromeliads actually catch and store rainwater in which insects and frogs may live.

Glades Animals. Everglades National Park was created primarily in an effort to save the egret, heron, ibis, roseate spoonbill, and other birds that were caught for their magnificent feathers. But the Glades is home to numerous species.

The American alligator is probably the most famous Glades resident. When the water level falls during the winter dry season, alligators dig their own personal ponds in low places. Each animal returns to its same hole each year, gradually making it bigger and deeper. Snails, frogs, snakes, and fish can survive in these gator holes during dry periods. When summer rains come and the water level rises, the alligators reproduce. The female may guard as many as 50 or 60 eggs at a time, while the heat of the sun and of vegetation fermenting incubate the eggs. When the water is high, alligators can be seen everywhere, even in roadside ditches.

Poisonous snakes lurk in the Everglades. The diamondback rattlesnake grows up to 6 feet (1.8 meters) long. The cottonmouth and water moccasin also live in the swamp, but

The coastal swamps in the Everglades include many mangroves (left), which have roots that prop them above the water, as if the trees were on stilts. Other kinds of Everglades plants include epiphytes such as this orchid (above).

they rarely bother people. The box turtle is the most common freshwater turtle. The loggerhead sea turtle lays its eggs on the coastal sand beaches.

Many water birds that pass through eastern North America spend some time in the Everglades. However, the region is best known for its egrets, great white herons, white ibises, and spoonbills (which have bright pink bodies, red legs, and spoon-shaped beaks). Ospreys, eagles, storks, and kites are among other large birds that live there.

When the water level is high, mammals and birds gather on the hammocks. White-tailed deer are increasing in number. The Glades deer are smaller and spend a lot of time in the water, wading between the hammocks.

The only panthers (also called cougars, mountain lions, and pumas) left on the East Coast reside in the Everglades—and they are almost gone.

Along the coast reside two of the most delightful sea mammals, the sea cow or manatee and the bottle-nosed dolphin or porpoise. They both move up into the coastal rivers from the Gulf of Mexico.

But this wondrous habitat is in danger. Much of what makes the Everglades so special has been hurt by people.

Changes Come to the Glades

In 1941, Marjory Stoneman Douglas published a wonderful book called *The Everglades: River of Grass,* which made the public aware of the national treasure they had in the Everglades. Six years later, the southern part of the Glades was established as Everglades National Park. But having government protection doesn't guarantee the preservation of the park, let alone the rest of the area.

When Everglades National Park was created, many animals were saved from extinction. Water birds such as the wood stork and the roseate spoonbill (above), and the snowy egret (bottom right) used to be killed for their feathers. The Glades' most famous resident, the American alligator (right), was hunted for its hide and meat. And the Florida manatee (below), a strange-looking mammal as long as 15 feet (4.5 meters), is safer in the Glades from death caused by motorboat propellers than in canals and rivers.

In recent years, Miami's growing population has needed drinking water. The new agricultural land north of the Everglades has required irrigating. Numerous levees and canals and dams were built to take the water from Lake Okeechobee and spread it everywhere except the Everglades. Less than half the water the Glades used to get now makes its way through the river of grass and swamps to the sea. In fact, the Everglades National Park relies solely on rainwater to replenish its swamps. Salt water poured into the coastal swamps, damaging the water in the aquifer below and harming the plants and animals.

In addition, much land south of Lake Okeechobee has been drained and turned into sugarcane fields. Runoff from the fields is high in nitrogen and phosphorus, which hurt some marsh plants and encourage others to grow. Cattails are also encouraged by the fact that much of the water stands unmoving now instead of rising and falling with the season. The cattail growth, along with excess algae, tend to choke out all other life.

The effects of all this? The Everglades is shrinking. At least 90 percent of the wading birds that called it home have disappeared. More than a dozen species of animals are on the endangered list, including the manatee, panther, crocodile, snail kite, wood stork, and five species of sea turtles.

Rescuing the Everglades

In 1989, the federal government sued the state of Florida, calling for the state to enforce

The canal systems around the Everglades diverted the natural water flow. These water projects helped farming expand and the Everglades shrink.

water quality standards to save the Everglades before it was too late. It took time, but in May 1991, the Florida legislature passed the Marjory Stoneman Douglas Everglades Protection Act to rehabilitate the Everglades. Two months later, the federal and state governments signed an agreement.

The state of Florida will build a system of four constructed wetlands (described in the next chapter) that will filter the nutrients from agricultural stormwater runoff before it enters the Everglades. The filtering marshes will occupy 32,600 acres (13,190 hectares). Ground was broken for the first artificial marsh in August 1991. If they are not doing their job fully by 2002, the state must contribute up to 36,000 acres (14,570 hectares) more to artificial marshes.

Farmers who, in the past, have released their stormwater runoff immediately into the water reaching the Everglades must now hold runoff back as long as possible, keeping the phosphorus on their own lands. This requirement will not hurt the sugarcane crops because cane can grow in water. But the area also supports numerous vegetable farms, where standing water would be harmful. They will have to develop cooperative plans with the sugarcane farmers by which the farmers would take the water.

The constructed wetlands will also supply adequate amounts of water to maintain and restore the natural abundance and variety of plants and animals in the Everglades and nearby Loxhatchee National Wildlife Refuge.

New artificial wetlands will thus rehabilitate natural, misused ones. Perhaps human ideas and ingenuity can help one of the great wetland treasures of the world to begin rebuilding itself before it is too late. Maybe this is a new beginning for the Everglades story.

Chapter 7

Wetlands for the Future

THE ARCATA MARSH and Wildlife Sanctuary lies in a small university town in a redwood area on the coast north of San Francisco. Many people visit this beautiful 94-acre (38-hectare) area of saltwater and freshwater marshes. Over 150 species of birds, permanent and migratory, feed on insect larvae, tadpoles, and plants. Duckweed and algae are plentiful. What some visitors don't know, however, is that the community of Arcata routes its wastewater through the sanctuary.

In 1977, the sanctuary area consisted of an old dump, an abandoned lumber mill, and an old railway bridge. Then the state of California announced its intention to build a huge, expensive sewage-treatment plant in Arcata. The town would have to stop dumping their wastewater into Humboldt Bay or meet state water-quality standards before doing so. The citizens said no, they didn't want the treatment plant. But they had to find a way to meet state standards.

A college student came up with the answer. Why not pass the local wastewater through the wetlands? That seemed a rather strange idea at first, but gradually a plan was developed that combined the use of a sewage-treatment plant with man-made, or constructed, marshes.

Using heavy equipment, workers removed the topsoil and began to form the land. When the site was ready, the topsoil was returned to the site and water was let in. No seeding was done. Nature took care of supplying the vegetation. Slowly, the land took on the appearance and functions of a marsh.

The people of Arcata now feed their wastewater into the 94-acre marshland. The root hairs of marsh plants attract particles of raw sewage. Bacteria living near the roots break

down the raw sewage into harmless chemicals. The end result is cleaner water released into Humboldt Bay and food for the marsh plants. And the Arcata Marsh and Wildlife Sanctuary provides new habitat for wildlife.

Constructed Marshes

Building a marsh to treat sewage didn't begin in California. It was first proposed by Kate Seidel of the Max Planck Institute in Germany in the 1950s. In the United States, Dr. William Wolverton researched the idea at the National Space Technology Laboratories in Mississippi twenty years later. In the 1980s, waste treatment by marsh became accepted, and several hundred wetlands in Canada, the United States, and Europe have been constructed as natural sewage-disposal sites. Special wetlands used for cleaning wastewater usually are constructed because it is illegal to deliberately let pollutants go into wetland.

A constructed wetland can be built as small as one needed to replace a septic system for an individual home or large enough to treat the waste from an entire city. Some large marshes can purify as much as 20 million gallons (75 million liters) of raw waste daily. There are now also wetlands that treat wastewater from industries such as mining, textiles, paper pulp, as well as runoff from farms and towns.

A Constructed Wetland

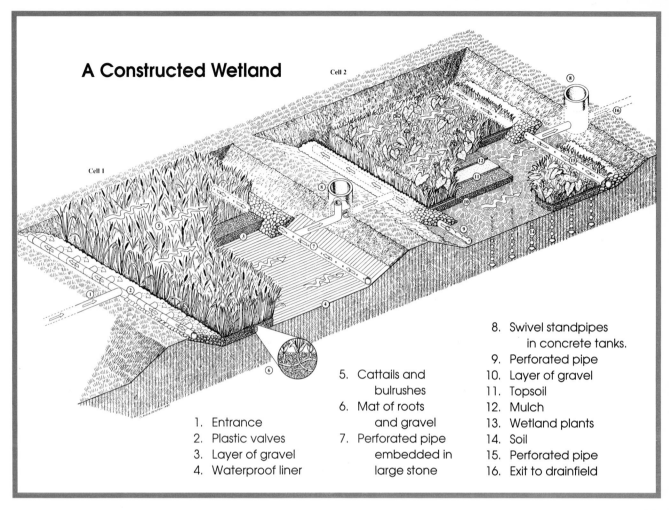

Cell 2

Cell 1

1. Entrance
2. Plastic valves
3. Layer of gravel
4. Waterproof liner
5. Cattails and bulrushes
6. Mat of roots and gravel
7. Perforated pipe embedded in large stone
8. Swivel standpipes in concrete tanks.
9. Perforated pipe
10. Layer of gravel
11. Topsoil
12. Mulch
13. Wetland plants
14. Soil
15. Perforated pipe
16. Exit to drainfield

Making a Marsh. Simple systems for homes and small businesses may consist of just two sections, called cells. The first has gravel and a plastic liner on the bottom. It may be planted with cattails and bulrushes. Plants native to the region are always used. Physical, chemical, and biological processes take place in that cell before the water moves on. The second cell also has a gravel bottom but no liner. It is planted with more ornamental plants such as iris and arrowhead, which do some further cleaning before the water, much cleaner than when it entered, seeps down into the ground.

99

Marshes can be designed small enough to clean wastewater from a single family home.

Industrial Waste. The waste need not be just sewage from homes and businesses. In fact, wetlands have proved to be quite efficient at removing chemicals, as well as such heavy metals as cadmium and mercury, from industrial waste.

The U.S. Bureau of Mines is creating marshes to help clean up water polluted by the coal-mining process. More than 5,000 miles (8,000 kilometers) of rivers and streams in Appalachia have been contaminated.

When coal is exposed during strip mining, the mineral pyrite, or fool's gold, is exposed. It contains a large amount of sulfur and iron. Rain and air change this sulfur to sulfuric acid. The acid gets washed into waterways where the acidity may be high enough to kill fish and wildlife and harm farm animals.

In 1977, the coal industry was ordered to restore the regions that had been mined to an "acceptable" state. A government researcher noticed that when mine wastewater flowed through natural wetlands, the pollution was significantly decreased. Mining companies decided that new wetlands could be built and planted to handle polluted drainage water. Over 300 cattail marshes have been constructed so far to do the mining cleanup.

One main difference between a constructed wetland and

a natural one is in the way the water flows through it. In a natural marsh or swamp, the water is mostly confined to channels. In a man-made wetland, the water is spread evenly throughout the system. Another difference is that not as much water can seep into the groundwater below.

Depending on location, the type of wastewater to be treated, and some other factors, the construction of wetlands to clean wastewater costs only one-tenth to one-twelfth as much as traditional treatment plants, and a well-designed system will maintain itself.

Can Humans Really Create New Wetlands?

Yes and no.

Dr. Joy Zedler, a San Diego State University biologist, says, "We are learning how to plant wetland gardens, but we don't know if we can create wetland ecosystems."

The U.S. government has a requirement for mitigation which is constructing new wetlands to replace ones lost to development. So many people have had experience with trying to make new wetlands, but constructed marshes haven't been around long enough to know for sure what the final results will be. It takes careful planning and considerable time and money. After many years the area *may* become a natural community.

A new marsh can be left to seed itself, as Arcata was, or seeds from existing marsh plants can be sown. Marsh seeds tend to grow quickly when given water because they have evolved to take advantage of the changes from dry to wet periods. There are now a number of companies around the country that specialize in supplying wetland plants to builders and industrial plant owners who are trying to do the

Planting reeds in a new marsh is fairly easy, but creating a complete wetland ecosystem is a more difficult task. So far nature does a better job than humans.

right thing with the property they are building on.

Attracting animals to a new wetland site takes time, but they will find it. In the years following completion of the Arcata marsh, more than 200 species of birds appeared. The tall grasses along the bank will attract ducks for their nesting sites. Feeding and nesting structures for birds can be added. The water can be stocked with a variety of native fish. Amphibians and reptiles can be purchased and released into the new environment.

We can't duplicate all the beneficial functions of a wetland ecosystem. Those functions we can duplicate somewhat include improving water quality, storing floodwaters and releasing them slowly, and trapping sediments. There may be future problems with constructed wetlands that we don't know anything about yet. It's possible, for example, that a wetland treatment system may eventually become overloaded. It would reach the point at which it could not take any more waste without becoming polluted. What happens then? Nature still knows a lot more than humans do about how wetlands function best.

Preserving What We Have

Obviously, it is best to preserve the wetlands we have instead of depending on building new ones. Deforestation has damaged a lot of floodplains, but it is possible for the floodplains to be brought back as productive wetlands.

In the African country of Mali, for example, the Niger River regularly floods an area of 11,500 square miles (29,785 square kilometers) on the edge of the Sahara Desert. The fertile sediments that are deposited during the flood produce an abundant growth of grasses, which attract millions of birds. It also attracts native people who bring their cattle to graze. The animals' sharp hooves chop up the ground like plows. Their excrement fertilizes the soil.

That's the way it should be. But all too often, the cattle come into the area before the grasses have a chance to grow. If they are brought too late, the ground is so hard that the plants have withered.

Rather than turn the fertile ground into cropland as many people wished, the government of Mali has chosen to preserve its wetland. Outside organizations have come to help replant the trees on the wetland so that it will benefit everyone—wildlife, domestic cattle, and people.

Many countries are reducing deforestation, especially on floodplains. Millions of trees are being planted in areas that need them. Biologists have discovered that if woody plants won't germinate of their own accord in a wetland area, it is possible to encourage seeds of some species to germinate or roots to grow by temporarily holding back the water that flows into the wetland. Such water management is called drawdown. It has the added advantage of letting oxygen get into soil that is otherwise soggy and lacking oxygen.

Farmers that use "no-till" farming not only help stop soil erosion, but also provide good nesting sites for waterfowl and birds.

Better Farming Practices. A number of farmers have accepted that their own farming practices may be at fault in destroying wetlands and are doing something about it. One Indiana farmer, for example, practices "no-till" farming in his corn and soybean fields. This means that the soil does not get loosened, which would let it be carried away with runoff or blown away by wind. In addition, he doesn't plant the same crops every year. Instead, he rotates them. Crop rotation has the side effect of preventing the build-up of pests that attack certain plants. Therefore, he doesn't need pesticides at all. So there's no chemical runoff to wetland areas.

He has left his wetlands for the waterfowl and wildlife. He has abandoned "modern" farming to protect and enhance his wetlands and his whole way of life.

The Cheyenne Bottoms Story

In 1970, Jan Garton, a college student from Manhattan, Kansas, visited the nearby Cheyenne Bottoms Wildlife Area, a 19,000-acre (7,690-hectare) wetland, for the first time. She was not impressed. It seemed flat and uninteresting. But then she found out that it was the most important stopping point for shorebirds migrating in the Central Flyway. About 45 percent of all North American shorebirds use the Bottoms, and more than 90 percent of the population of five individual species depend on it during their migrations. Hundreds of thousands of waterfowl stop in the Bottoms to feed and rest. In fact, the area is crucial to the survival of the least tern, which is on the endangered list.

But in the early 1980s, the Cheyenne Bottoms was drying up because its main water source, the Arkansas River, was shrinking as its water was removed to irrigate crops. The wetland was receiving less than 10 percent of the water it was entitled to.

Jan Garton became concerned and set about organizing a conference of conservationists and state officials to try to solve the problem. They worked together in a partnership. The Cheyenne Bottoms is still vulnerable, but enough water is getting to it now to save the wetland and the wildlife.

The Cheyenne Bottoms probably could not have been saved by government officials making rules or even by environmentally concerned organizations. But it was saved by a partnership among government, organizations, and individuals. Such partnerships are the best hope for the future of the wetlands.

Shorebirds migrating in the Central Flyway can still find a resting place at Cheyenne Bottoms on the Arkansas River because Jan Garton worked to save its vital wetlands.

The Canadian Situation

Because North America has a shorter recorded history than other continents, the destruction of wetlands is more easily recognized here than in Europe or Asia. Fortunately, we are recognizing the destruction and trying to do something about it before it's too late.

Canada is particularly in need of partnerships among government and private organizations and industry because there is no central agency to manage wetlands. All wetlands have been managed through provincial governments.

Efforts are now underway to create a federal policy that will encourage voluntary partnerships for conservation. The Canadian National Task Force is in charge of this policy. However, no single piece of legislation for wetland regulation or activities occurring in or near wetland habitats is in force at present.

Bringing Back Waterfowl

"There are some very special places
Where time stands still,
And waterfowl wings whistle
In the half-light before dawn."

Biologists, hunters, and birdwatchers have been noticing since the 1970s that there are fewer and fewer wings whis-

The early Acadian settlers of Nova Scotia, Canada, diked the Bay of Fundy wetlands for farming. Many of the original wetlands are being re-established through Canada's support of the North American Wildlife Management Plan.

106

Prairie Habitat
Pacific Coast
Prairie Pothole
Eastern Habitat
Lower Great Lakes/ St. Lawrence Basin
Atlantic Coast
Central Valley
Rainwater Basin
Playa Lakes
Gulf Coast
Lower Mississippi Valley
Current Joint Venture Area
1992-95 Joint Venture Area

tling, that the waterfowl population of North America has been drastically shrinking. Where hundreds of millions of birds used to migrate north, the numbers have dropped in recent years to a few million or less as more and more wetland habitat—the "very special places"—was destroyed.

In 1986, the Canadian and United States governments formed the North American Waterfowl Management Plan (NAWMP) to protect and rehabilitate at least 6 million acres (2.4 million hectares) of wetland for the purpose of increasing the numbers of waterfowl. The plan is to achieve a breeding duck population of 62 million birds, so that autumn migration will include at least 100 million ducks.

In 1989, Mexico joined the partnership. Wetlands in Mexico are important as wintering habitats for birds that breed in the United States and Canada, such as pintails, redheads, brant geese, and others whose numbers have been going down throughout North America. Many of Mexico's

NAWMP's goals include the management of wetland habitat in eleven large areas of North America.

wetlands are being affected by pollution, development, and agricultural activities. This damage affects the birds of the entire continent.

NAWMP works through Joint Ventures, which are partnerships of government, corporations, individuals, and private organizations. In one typical Joint Venture project, volunteers, including the owner of a crop-dusting service, sowed 23 tons (20.7 metric tons) of millet and other seed in the exposed mudflats around Big Lake in northern Arkansas. The crop of grasses was grown in time for their seeds to attract almost a million ducks during the winter—thirty times the number that had arrived the previous year.

The United States Government

In the 1960s, Americans started to wonder if all the huge government projects to shift water here or there were really good. Things started to change after the passage of the Clean Water Act of 1972. This law was really the beginning of the U.S. national wetlands policy. It is the responsibility of the Corps of Engineers to regulate discharge of dredged or fill material into American waters and to control point-source pollutant discharges into water. Anyone planning to alter a wetland area or discharge anything into a body of water must have a permit from the Corps of Engineers. Unfortunately, such permits are rarely turned down.

Offsetting Wetland Loss. The law also requires that when a wetland is changed in some harmful way, that change must be offset, or *mitigated*, by fixing up another wetland area. For example, if your family wanted to build a house on a piece of wetland that would have to be dredged or

The U.S. Army Corps of Engineers is changing from builders to regulators and protectors of U.S. aquatic ecosystems. Calhoun Point, where the Mississippi and Illinois Rivers meet, is being restored as waterfowl habitat.

filled, you would have to get a permit from the U.S. Army Corps of Engineers. If you needed a house of a certain size and that size could be achieved only by building on the wet area, they might approve the permit only if you could build a new wetland of the same kind right in the same vicinity.

Developers planning to fill in only 1 to 10 acres (0.4 to 4 hectares) of wetland don't require a permit, so some developers are now dividing their large fill operations into pieces of 9.9 acres (3.96 hectares) or less. That way they don't have to notify the Corps of Engineers or have a permit.

FACT

The city of Hazelton, West Virginia, wanted to expand its existing reservoir by enlarging a dam that would flood wetlands. In order to mitigate the loss, the city was told to create a wetland next to the reservoir. Hazelton built their new wetland, but every time a corps inspector came by, the water to the area had been turned off and the plants were dead. The government is still trying to get Hazelton to comply with the conditions of the permit.

The Environmental Protection Agency can override a decision of the Corps of Engineers, but there has been little consistency in the way that power is used. A number of bills are currently in Congress that would clarify the control over wetlands, though most of them would allow more to be destroyed than have been in recent years.

FACT

The EPA requires that there must be a 1 ½ times replacement for any wetlands destroyed. But there are often loopholes that uncaring people use to avoid meeting that requirement. In New Orleans, the effects of a new 2,500-acre (1,100-hectare) golf course built on wetland were "mitigated" by the construction of a small swampy park with a boardwalk running through it.

The U.S. Department of Agriculture (USDA) is also involved in wetlands. Since 1933, the federal government has paid farmers money called "price supports" that raise the prices they receive for their crops. This helps farmers make a more stable, predictable income. The USDA also can tell farmers how much land they can plant for certain crops.

This involvement of the government has speeded up wetland conversion and degradation. A farmer gets more money if he produces more, so farmers were encouraged to use larger amounts of pesticides and fertilizers and to fill potholes and plant in floodplains.

In 1985, Congress passed the Food Security Act, containing what has been called the "swampbuster" provision. This law says if any farmer drains or fills a wetland, or if he produces a crop on such land, he will lose any government payments for insurance or price supports to which he is entitled. This law is slowing down wetland destruction.

The U.S. Fish and Wildlife Service is involved heavily in wetlands because the laws protecting endangered species authorize that agency to buy wetland areas for the purpose of saving endangered plants and animals. As of 1990, 2 million acres (0.8 million hectares) of wetlands have been purchased by the United States government and added to the National Wildlife Refuge System. The system now includes more than 10 million acres (4 million hectares) where animals are protected.

Getting to Know the Estuaries. In 1972, the National Estuarine Sanctuary Program was established. It later had its name changed to National Estuarine Reserve Research System but its purpose remained the same: to help states help scientists acquire and develop estuaries for study, so that these areas could not all be harmed by the rapid development of beautiful coastal areas. It wasn't so much to preserve estuaries as to allow scientists an opportunity to study representative samples. What they learned in these natural laboratories would be useful for all people in and near those productive, but endangered, tidal places where rivers meet the sea.

Since 1974, wetland areas covering a total of 243,376 acres (98,490 hectares) have been incorporated in the Federal Estuarine Reserve Research Program. Only one of the areas—Old Woman Creek (left)—is a rare, freshwater estuary where the American lotus lives.

National Estuarine Reserve Research System

Padilla Bay
South Slough
Wells
Great Bay
Waquoit Bay
Narragansett Bay
Hudson Bay
Old Woman Creek
Chesapeake Bay, MD
Chesapeake Bay, VA
North Carolina
Elkhorn Slough
Tijuana River
Sapelo Island
Weeks Bay
Apalachicola
Waimanu Valley, HI
Rookery Bay

"No Net Loss." In recent years, the federal government policy was "no net loss" of wetlands, meaning that if a construction company or a farmer acquired a permit to fill in or drain some wetland, the land had to be replaced with an equal amount of wetland somewhere else. This meant that someone who had a piece of wetland and wanted to build a house on it would have to buy similar piece to turn into a wetland. Not many people could afford to do that.

And no one was completely sure just how the term "wetland" should be defined. At that time, the government was defining "wetland" as almost any area that was wet for even a few days during the growing season. A lot of land that scientists called wet appeared to the owners to be dry.

The White House changed the working partnership between the Corps and the EPA in February 1990 to take away mitigation requirements in areas where "there is a high proportion of land which is wetland." This "loophole" is designed to allow development of Alaska's tundra.

In August 1991, President George Bush announced a change in the definition of "wetland" that would release millions of acres to development. Many farmers and construction-company officials were elated by the decision, but most conservationists were dismayed. The new definition says that to be wetland, an area must have standing water on it for 15 straight days and be saturated down to 12 inches deep (30 centimeters) for at least 21 days. It also includes as wetlands only those areas containing plants that do not also grow on dry land.

The new definitions are still being reviewed and are not yet official policy. If it becomes policy, it will take time to see just what the actual effect on America's wetlands will be.

RAMSAR SITES IN THE U.S. AND CANADA

United States	Acres
The Everglades	1,399,000
Okefenokee Natl. Wildlife Ref. (swamp)	395,000
Chesapeake Bay (estuary)	111,000
Cheyenne Bottoms (floodplains)	10,000

Canada	
Quill Lakes	157,000
Peace-Athabasca Delta	794,000
Southern James Bay	62,000
Polar Bear Provincial Park (peatlands)	5,952,000
Queen Maud Gulf	15,320,000
Whooping Crane Summer Range (marshes, ponds, bogs)	4,175,000
Dewey Soper Migratory Bird Sanctuary (marshes and ponds)	2,016,000

Lake Nakuru, Kenya was designated as a Ramsar site in 1990. Large flocks of flamingos (sometimes several million birds) feed on crustaceans and mollusks in the shallow wetlands.

Hands Across the Wetlands

An agreement among nations called Ramsar began in 1971 when the Convention on Wetlands of International Importance was held in Ramsar, Iran. Sixty-one countries have signed the agreement. It specifies wetland areas within each country that are important to the entire world. Each nation is responsible for trying to preserve its own areas. The smallest is only 2.5 acres (1 hectare), on Christmas Island in Australia. The largest is also in Australia—most of Arnhem Land in the northern part of the continent.

Canada is blessed with many wetland areas. Its 30 Ramsar sites cover the largest acreage of any country—about 32 million acres (12.9 million hectares). Presently about 500 such wetlands—about 78 million acres (31 million hectares)—are being protected around the world.

Fortunately for ourselves and the wildlife around us, we are finding new ways to utilize and protect the marshes, swamps, and bogs of our planet. Now we know that instead of wastelands, wetlands are richlands, and it is up to all of us, working together, to treasure our wetlands for the future.

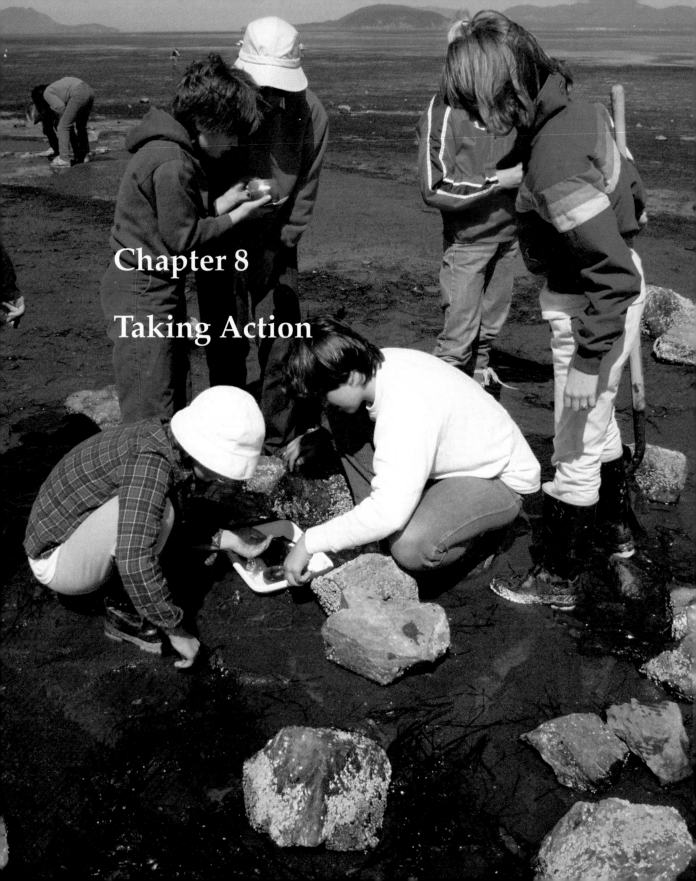

Chapter 8

Taking Action

WETLANDS AFFECT ALL OF US, and the things we do, want, and need affect the wetlands. There are many actions you can take—and many actions you can refrain from taking—that can have an impact on the marshes, swamps, and bogs that are such an important part of our lives.

Things to Do

1. Visit one of the nearly 400 National Wildlife Refuges in the United States or the similar parks and refuges in Canada. There, environmental education specialists often describe to visitors resident wildlife, its needs, and management.

2. If you live on the coasts, visit one of the National Estuarine Reserve Research Areas near you. Educational programs, tours, and workshops may be given.

3. Most states and provinces have programs to protect animals and plants that are rare or endangered in the area. Write your state or provincial fish and game/natural resources department to find out which species are rare in your area and what is being done to protect them.

4. Purchase federal duck stamps from your post office. Money from these sales is used to purchase wetlands around the country. Most states also have their own duck stamps.

5. Participate in the Federal Junior Duck Stamp Conservation Program by entering the stamp design contest.

6. If you live near a waterway, make a survey of what is being dumped into it and by whom. Are there toxic wastes from factories? Are the farms bordering the water using pesticides and heavy doses of commercial fertilizers? Do the storm sewers feed into the water? If you see anybody violating the waters, report it to the town or county authorities.

Past winner of a junior duck stamp design contest held each year. For information on participating, write the U.S. Department of the Interior, U.S. Fish and Wildlife Service, 1849 C St., NW, Washington, DC 20240.

7. If you live in a rural area and you see a "Swampbuster" violation, report it to the U.S. Dept. of Agriculture, tollfree number: 1-800-424-9121.

8. Pressure officials to use sand instead of salt on icy streets and highways. Freshwater plants and animals cannot live with the saltwater runoff.

9. Find out how much fertilizer and pesticides are used on your parks, recreational areas, and parkways. Encourage officials to cut back.

10. Build artificial nest sites for aquatic birds. A shallow, wooden box filled with dried grasses will attract mallards. Add a wooden platform around it on which a flying bird can land. Mount the box on a pole that you drive into the ground at the edge of a marsh or swamp. An almost closed box mounted vertically will attract wood ducks and goldeneyes.

11. Set up displays in your school, public library, or city hall explaining the importance and destruction of wetlands. This can help get the community to act on the problem.

12. Landowners who want to preserve wetlands can lease or sell wetlands to an organization such as a private hunting club, conservation club, or an organization such as Ducks Unlimited or the Nature Conservancy.

Things NOT to Do

1. Do not use (or at least reduce your use of) pesticides, herbicides, or other harmful chemicals that your family uses inside or outside the home. These eventually end up in our waterways, affecting the wildlife.

2. Do not let anyone in your family throw motor oil, paint, or cleaners down a sewer. They will end up in streams that feed the wetlands.

3. Do not buy exotic tropical fish. Divers who capture them for sale often damage other living organisms in the coral reefs or estuaries where the fish live. Also, do not release such fish into natural wetlands.

4. Do not waste water or electricity. The processes of purifying water and making electricity cause pollution in waterways and wetlands.

5. Never purchase jewelry or ornaments made of coral, dried seahorses, or rare shells. If people stop buying them, people who sell them will stop collecting them.

Many private citizens, farmers, and interested groups build nest baskets for birds and waterfowl. The eggs are safe from predators and most are able to hatch.

Stay Informed

1. Most city councils conduct open meetings. Encourage your parents to attend, and attend yourself if the issue of saving or permitting development or dumping in a wetland in your town is on the agenda. Wetlands are lost an acre at a time, so real impact can be at the local level—where we live. County commissions and city councils determine the fate of many wetland areas every day when they consider zoning changes. Be aware of what changes are being made.

2. Visit the sewage-disposal plant in your town. How effective is it? Where is the treated wastewater released when it leaves the plant?

3. Follow the discussions and decisions of the United States Congress or Canadian Parliament that are related to wetland protection or destruction. Write your representative when a controversial issue surfaces (see the list below). The

National Audubon Society runs a hotline providing up-to-date information on legislative actions: 202-547-9017. Be sure to get your parents' permission before calling. The EPA runs a tollfree Wetlands Hotline: 1-800-832-7828.

Writing Letters. In writing a letter to express your opinion on controversial issues, follow these tips:

1. Make your letter one page or less. Cover only one subject in each letter.

2. Introduce yourself and tell why you, personally, are for or against the issue.

3. Be clear and to the point.

4. Be specific on whether you want the person to vote "yes" or "no."

5. Write as an individual. The environmental groups you belong to will have already let the legislator know their stand on the issue.

6. When you get a response, write a follow-up letter to re-emphasize your position and give your reaction to your legislator's comments.

On issues concerning state legislation or to express your opinion about actions taken by your state or provincial environmental or natural resources agency, you can write to:

Your local state or provincial legislator. Check at your local library to discover his or her name.

The governor of your state or premier of your province. Write in care of your state or provincial capital.

The director of your state or province's department of natural resources or related environmental agency. Check your local library for the specific person and the address.

On issues concerning federal legislation or to express your opinion about actions taken by the federal government, you can write to:

Your two state senators. Check at your local library to discover their names.

> The Honorable _____
> U.S. Senate
> Washington, DC 20510

Your local congressman. Check at your local library to discover his or her name.

> The Honorable _____
> U.S. House of Representatives
> Washington, DC 20515

Your local provincial or federal member of Parliament. Check at your local library to discover his or her name.

> The Honorable _____
> House of Commons
> Ottawa, Ontario, Canada K1A 0Ao

The President of the United States. He has the power to veto, or turn down, bills approved by the Senate and the House of Representatives as well as to introduce bills of his own. He also has final control over what the U.S. Environmental Protection Agency and other agencies do.

> President _____
> The White House
> 1600 Pennsylvania Avenue, NW
> Washington, DC 20501

The Prime Minister of Canada.

> The Honorable _____
> House of Commons
> Ottawa, Ontario, Canada K1A 0A6

Participate

1. Be a Wetland Watchdog. The National Wildlife Federation has started programs in several states. Volunteers keep their eyes open for projects that may alter the wetlands. Community action is working.

2. Join the Audubon Activist Network. It will help get a group started in your community. A monthly news journal will keep you up-to-date on wetland concerns, problems, and issues. Over 20,000 concerned citizens have already joined to help.

3. Be an acid rain watcher. The National Audubon Society has organized groups all over the country to keep an eye on our water and land habitats. Each week you would collect rain or snow to be tested with pH measuring paper. Data collected by local clubs is fed into a state organization. This could provide grounds for action against the people who pollute our air.

4. Support and contribute to the Chesapeake Bay Foundation, Coast Alliance, Center for Marine Conservation, World Wildlife Fund, or any of the other organizations listed below. A number of them, but especially The Nature Conservancy, actually buy up endangered places so that they can be protected.

The following organizations are among those that play a major role in preserving wetlands:

Canadian Nature Federation, 453 Sussex Drive, Ottawa, Ontario, Canada K1N 6Z4

Canadian Wildlife Federation, 1673 Carling Ave., Ottawa, Ontario, Canada K2A 3Z1

Center for Marine Conservation, 1725 DeSales St., Suite 500, NW, Washington, DC 20036

Chesapeake Bay Foundation, 162 Prince George St., Annapolis, MD 21401

Coast Alliance, 1536 16th St., NW, Washington, DC 20036

Defenders of Wildlife, 1244 19th St., NW, Washington, DC 20036

Ducks Unlimited, One Waterfowl Way, Long Grove, IL 60047, or 1190 Waverley St., Winnipeg, Manitoba, Canada R3T 2E2

Environmental Defense Fund, 1616 P St., NW, Washington, DC 20036

Environmental Law Institute, 1616 P St., NW, Washington, DC 20036

Greenpeace USA, 1436 U St., NW, Washington, DC 20009

National Audubon Society, 950 Third Ave., New York, NY 10022

National Wildlife Federation, 1400 16th St., NW, Washington, DC 20036

Natural Resources Defense Council, 1350 New York Avenue, NW, #300, Washington, DC 20005

The Nature Conservancy, 1815 N. Lynn St., Arlington, VA 22209

The Sierra Club, 730 Polk St., San Francisco, CA 94109

Wilderness Society, 1400 I St., NW, 10th Floor, Washington, DC 20005

Wildlife Habitat Canada, 1704 Carling Ave., #301, Ottawa, Ontario, Canada K2A 1C7

World Wildlife Fund, 1250 24th St., NW, Washington, DC 20037, or 60 St. Clair Ave., E., Suite 201, Toronto, Ontario, Canada M4T 1N5

Worldwatch Institute, 1776 Massachusetts Ave., NW, Washington, DC 20036

Each of us needs to remain aware of what others do to the Earth around us. The Supreme Court of the State of Wisconsin has said:

The land belongs to the people . . . a little of it to those dead . . . some to those living . . . but most of it belongs to those yet to be born . . . . An owner of land has no absolute and unlimited right to change the essential natural character of his land so as to use it for a purpose for which it was unsuited in its natural state and which injures the rights of others.

GLOSSARY

acid rain — precipitation that contains a concentration of sulfuric acid, nitric acid, and other chemicals.

algae — the simplest of green plants that can make their own food. They may be single-celled, filamentous, or colonial.

aquifer — a water-bearing rock formation below the water table where all the pores between particles of rock are filled with water.

bay — a water body formed along the coast, an inlet or indentation from the straight shoreline. It is much smaller than a gulf but larger than a cove.

biomass — the total weight of living organisms in a given space at one time. In relation to energy, it refers to the once-living material as fuel.

carbon (C) — an element found in living organisms, fossil fuels, and in the air; combines with oxygen to form carbon dioxide (CO_2).

calorie — a unit of heat used to measure the energy value of food. It is the amount of heat required to raise the temperature of 2.2 pounds (1 kilogram) of water 1 degree Celsius.

crustacean — a class of animals in the Phylum Arthropoda. Most have a shell or exoskeleton. Includes crab, lobster, crayfish, and daphnia.

dam — a structure or barrier built of soil, concrete, or other material to stop the flow of water in a stream, river, or similar waterway.

decomposition — the breakdown of complex materials into simpler substances. Once-living organisms are decomposed by fungi and bacteria.

detritus — partially decomposed organic matter that serves as food for animals low on the food chain.

dredge — to use a machine to scoop out the sediment at the bottom of a river channel or lake.

dike — a lengthwise bank of earth used to control the waters of a stream, river, or ocean.

ecosystem — a group of living organisms interacting with and in a certain physical environment.

EPA — see **United States Environmental Protection Agency**

erosion — the wearing away of the Earth's surface by wind, water, or ice.

eutrophication — the enrichment of a body of water (lake, pond, marsh) with nutrients, causing it to become a different community. This change, or succession, may be natural or caused by humans.

global warming — the heating up of planet Earth over a period of time, primarily caused by the addition of too many heat-trapping gases to the atmosphere, causing the greenhouse effect to work beyond usual limits.

greenhouse effect — the trapping of the sun's heat in Earth's atmosphere by molecules of certain gases, particularly carbon dioxide, causing Earth's temperature to be warm.

groundwater — water deep in the ground but above the underlying, impenetrable rock. In low-lying places it forms ponds and marshes. At higher elevations, it is reached only by wells.

habitat — the total environment in which a plant or animal lives, providing food, water, space, and protection; its "home address."

hydrology — the movement of water in or near the surface of soil. Also, the study of water and its movement through the Earth.

invertebrate — an animal without a backbone or vertebral column, such as insects and shellfish.

kettle — a depression, usually circular, in the ground formed when receding glaciers left chunks of ice in the soil; also called kettle hole.

levee — a bank or ridge of mud or sand that keeps a river or stream from flooding land on either side of it. It can also be an embankment to contain the water on land that humans want to be flooded.

methane (CH$_4$) — an odorless gas formed by organic material decomposing as in a marsh.

nitrate (NO$_3$) — a compound containing nitrogen in a form that can be used by green plants.

nitrogen (N) — a gas that has no odor or color. It makes up 78 percent of the atmosphere. It is in combination with other elements in living cells.

nitrogen oxide (NO$_x$) — any of several colorless gases composed of nitrogen and oxygen. When combined with water, they form nitric acid, a component of acid rain.

ozone (O$_3$) — a gas formed by a reaction between nitrogen oxide and hydrocarbons in the presence of sunshine. In the upper atmosphere it contributes to protecting life from harmful ultraviolet radiation.

pesticide — a chemical used to kill such pests as weeds, fungi, insects, or rodents.

pH — letters standing for potential hydrogen, used to indicate the degree of acidity or alkalinity of a substance. On a scale from 0 to 14, 7 is neutral, lower numbers indicate an acid substance and higher an alkaline or basic.

phosphorus (P) — an element used as a fertilizer. It has a vital part in the functioning of all living cells.

photosynthesis — the making of sugar by green plants from water and carbon dioxide in the presence of light: oxygen is a by-product.

productivity — the amount of energy that accumulates in a plant through the process of photosynthesis. This energy is in the form of stored carbohydrates, proteins, and/or oils.

reservoir — the body of water behind a constructed dam. Water is stored to use for hydroelectric power, irrigation, or city water supplies.

salinity — the saltiness of a substance.

sediment — any material, previously suspended in water, that settles out of the water onto a surface.

sludge — the material that settles out when wastewater is treated in a disposal plant.

spawn — the eggs or the laying of them in water by such aquatic animals as fish, crustaceans, and amphibians.

sulfur dioxide (SO$_2$) — a colorless gas composed of sulfur and oxygen which irritates lungs and corrodes metals. When it combines with water, it forms sulfuric acid, a component in acid rain.

United States Environmental Protection Agency — a federal government agency whose job is to regulate factors of the environment and those that may be affecting it.

watershed — the area of land drained by a stream, river, or other body of water.

water table — the top of the area underground where all spaces between soil and rock are completely filled with water.

See also page 41.

Index

Bold number = illustration

A

Acadians 57, **106**
acid rain 120, 122
acidic 8, 23, 24, 25, 28, 41, 100
aerial roots 28, **39**, 40; see also
   prop roots
agriculture **27**, 30, 46, 50, 51, 55-
   58, 62, 63, 90, 94, 95, **106**, 108
Alabama **72**
Alaska **11**, **17**, 86
Alatna River **11**
Alcock, John 22
algae **19**, 38, 66, 77, 78, 94, 122
alkaline 28
alluvial soil 57
American alligator 91, **93**
American crocodile 40, 94
American Indians 8
anaerobic 14, 23, 24
animals **20**, 25, 26, 32, 39, 40, 46,
   47, 92
Appalachia 100
aquaculture 53, 74, 75
aquatic plants 19, 66, 77, 78, 83,
   84
     Experience 66
Aransas National Wildlife
   Refuge 46
Arcata Marsh and Wildlife
   Sanctuary 97, **98**, 102
Arctic National Wildlife Refuge
   86
Arizona **70**
Arkansas 108
Arkansas River **105**
arsenic 63, 81
Asia **60**, 106
Atchafalaya River **64**
Australia 40, 75, 113

B

bacteria 23, 97
Ballona wetland 39

Bangladesh 40, 48, 52, 60
barrier islands **38**
bay 9, 33, 41, 80, 122
Bay of Fundy **106**
bayou 16, 41
beaver 18, 32, 46
Big Cypress Preserve 90
biomass 122
birds 13, 20, 26, 33, 36, 39, 40, 45,
   46, 47, 62, 73, 91, 92, 94, 102-
   105, 107, 108, 117
bog 7-9, 16, 18, **23**-26, 41, 53, 82,
   113
     Experience 23
bosques 41
bottomlands 41, 57
brackish 16, 33, 38, 39, 41, 47
breeding 11, 27, 40, 45, 46
British Columbia 87, 71
bromeliads 91
Brown, Arthur Whitten 22
Bush, President George 112

C

California 39, **62**, **63**, **70**, 86, 97
calories 59, 122
Canada 11, 26, 27, 32, **33**, 41, 44,
   45, 46, 57, 58, 71, 74, 82, 83, 87,
   98, 106, 107, 113, 115
Canada geese **9**
Canadian National Task Force
   106
canals 57, **65**, **67**, **86**, **94**
capybara **20**
carbon dioxide 19, 22, 86
carr 41
cattails 14-16, 19, 20, 41, 52, 94,
   99, 100
cattle 59, **60**, 68, 69, 103
channelization 62, 65, **67**, 66, 69
Charles River 43
chemicals 50, 77, 80, 81, 100
Chesapeake Bay 50, **52**, 113, 120,
   121
Cheyenne Bottoms Wildlife Area
   104, **105**, 113
clams 35, 53, 61, 85
Clean Water Act of 1972 108

coastal wetlands 10, 17, 33-40,
   41, 48, 49, 52, 69, 70-73, 86, **91**,
   94
Colorado River **70**
commercial fishing 53, 69, 75
constructed wetlands 96-103,
   109
crabs 35, 38, 40, 53
cranberries **25**, 53, 82
crayfish 20, 53
crop rotation 78, 104
crustaceans **35**, 113, 122
curlew **21**, 28, 39
cypress trees **12**, 28, 29, 90

D

dabbling ducks 44, **45**
dams 18, 30, 62, 63, **70**, 71, 83, 94,
   122
decomposition 23, 24, 122
deforestation 73, 75, 103
dehydration 83
delta 9, 31-**33**, 41, 55, 57, 61, 71
     Experience 32
Denmark 8
depressions 17, 18, **23**, 27, 41
Des Plaines River 72
detritus 35, 36, 122
Dewey Soper Migratory Bird
   Sanctuary 113
dikes 18, 57, 62, 65, **106**, 122
dissolved oxygen 22, 23, 28
     Experience 22
diving ducks 44
Douglas, Marjory Stoneman 92
draining wetlands 10, 55, **57**, 58,
   69, 73
drawdown 103
dredging 10, 64, 65, 108, 122
droughts **56**
duck stamps 44, 115, **116**
ducks 27, 44-46, 62, 69, 102, 107,
   108
DuPage River 72

E

eagles 36, 39, 73, 92
ecosystem 101, 102, 122

124

PHOTO SOURCES

Alabama Bureau of Tourism & Travel: 72
City of Arcata, California: 98
Board Failte Photo: 6, 26
The British Museum: 8
Bureau of Reclamation Photo by E.E. Hertzog: 70
California Department of Water Resources: 62
Canadian Wildlife Service—Environment Canada: 33, 46
Canadian Wildlife Service/Keith McAloney: 30, 106
Glen Chambers (Ducks Unlimited): 33, 56
Communi-graphics: 74
Jim Couch/Georgia Department of Natural Resources: 42, 93
Ducks Unlimited: 45
Ducks Unlimited Canada: 87
Florida Department of Natural Resources: 93
Food and Agriculture Organization/F. Mattioli: 79
Bob Harrington/Michigan Department of Natural Resources: 37
Carrol Henderson: 20, 37, 52, 54, 61
Larry Hyman/USFWS: 105, 113
Iowa Department of Natural Resources: 47
Photo by Gary Kramer: 93
Laidlaw Environmental Services, Inc.: 81
Helen Leitman/USGS: 29
Louisiana Department of Natural Resources/Office of Coastal Restoration and Management: 31, 58, 65, 69, 72, 86
Michigan Department of Natural Resources: 10
Courtesy Michigan Travel Bureau: 9
Courtesy Michigan Travel Bureau/Thomas A. Schneider: 2
Minnesota Department of Natural Resources: 17, 19, 57
Minnesota Department of Natural Resources Natural Heritage Program: 24
Minnesota Pollution Control Agency: 76
NASA: 31
National Marine Fisheries Service: 35, 47, 53, 75

National Oceanic & Atmospheric Administration/Sanctuaries and Reserve Division: 21, 34, 38, 40, 52, 93
National Park Service: 39, 90, 91, 94
National Park Service Photo by M. Woodbridge Williams: 11
The Nature Conservancy: 12, 13
Old Woman Creek National Estuarine Research Reserve: 111
Vicki Osis/OSU Marine Science Center: 36
Padilla Bay National Estuarine Research Reserve: 36, 114
Photo courtesy of Saskatchewan Wetland Conservation Corporation: 104, 117
South Florida Water Management District: 67, 68, 88
South Florida Water Management District/Pat Partington: 91, 93
Al Stenstrup: 20
Ralph Tiner/USFWS: 23, 82
TVA Water Quality Department: 15, 96, 100, 102
U.S. Army Corps of Engineers/New Orleans District: 64
U.S. Army Corps of Engineers/St. Louis District: 109
USDA-Soil Conservation Service: 25, 60
U.S. Fish and Wildlife Service: 27, 37, 45, 107, 116
USFWS/Matthew Perry: 27
Wisconsin Department of Natural Resources: 21, 48, 80
World Bank Photo Library: 60
USFWS Photo by Gary R. Zahm: 63

ILLUSTRATIONS

Jim McEvoy/Wisconsin Department of Natural Resources: 49, 51
Iowa State University Extension: 14
Ralph Tiner/USFWS: 15, 35
TVA Water Quality Department: 99

Permission to use the cattails symbol throughout this publication was granted by **Wildlife Habitat Canada**—a private foundation dedicated to conserving the great variety of wildlife habitats across Canada and publishers of Canada's conservation stamp.

ABOUT THE AUTHOR

Helen J. Challand is Professor of Science Education at National-Louis University (formerly National College of Education) in Evanston, Illinois. A nationally recognized authority on teaching science in the elementary grades, she has served as associate editor of the *Young People's Science Encyclopedia* and is the author of nine books of experiments for children. She is the author of all activities in the SAVING PLANET EARTH books and is the education consultant for the entire series. Dr. Challand lives in Shabbona, Illinois, not far from the forests and wetlands that she loves.